KILLER BLIZZARD

DAN JORGENSEN

MAJOR BOOKS • CANOGA PARK, CALIFORNIA

For Susan

Acknowledgement

Thanks to Bunny Jewert, Carolyn Amiet, and Dr. Kelvin F. Kesler, M.D., F.A.C.O.G., for their help and advice in the construction of this book.

PROLOGUE

A mild summer did not prepare the people of the upper Great Plains for the wrath of the winter that followed. It struck with a vengeance, hurling storm after storm at the wide-open prairie states. It had a devastating effect.

People died, stranded on their isolated farms or the long, open highways that serve as arteries across the Dakotas, Nebraska, Wyoming, and Montana. Thousands of cattle and sheep froze to death on the open rangelands, out of reach from the farmers and ranchers forced to sit tight near their homesteads because of the quantities of snow and the intense cold. Temperatures during some of the storms dropped as low as 35 below zero, and, coupled with the northern winds, wind chill factors of 85 below zero were not uncommon.

Old-timers compared it with the furious winters

of '97 and '98, and those of later years said it looked like the disastrous winters of the early '30s. Before it was over, more than 100 inches of snow were dumped on places where 30 was the norm.

The winter's true drama, however, came with its effect on the people. They struggled, fought, lived, and died in many ways.

This is the story of one group of people caught for a single day by a blizzard that winter; a few of them coped with it, others did not—but all had but a single purpose: to survive!

CHAPTER ONE

Lorre turned up the collar of his jacket as he passed the corner of the steam house. It was chilly and the wind was picking up. Fall was passing quickly and winter was just a breath away. He shivered slightly, perhaps more from the thought of the upcoming season rather than the present chill in the air.

Kicking halfheartedly at a small rock in his path, he stopped, leaned against the granite wall, and surveyed the courtyard. Here and there two or three men talked and laughed. A small group was playing a roughhouse form of touch football. Several others walked in twos and threes, some holding hands.

A typical day, he thought wryly, as far as prison days were concerned. It had been that same scene now for three years—three years that had seemed to drag on as if they were thirty, and inside he ached to walk out on any form of free ground he could find.

"Ready?"

Lorre started as the voice reached him, then relaxed as he turned to face his friend, Jack Schumacher. Friendships didn't come easy in prison, but he and Jack had hit it off. They shared a need for solitude. Now they were about to take their greatest risk together.

"Yeah, guess so," Lorre answered, glancing around the yard once more and shivering again. "How about Hernandez? Nothing's changed at his end, has it?"

"No. It's still set for nine-thirty. You get me that work slip?"

Lorre glanced quickly around, then pulled a yellow slip of paper from his coat and shoved it into Jack's pocket. "Come on," he said gruffly, "let's take a walk."

They started off along the wall, then veered out toward the courtyard's center, carefully eyeing the guard as they passed him. "Okay, let's hear it one more time."

"All right," Jack said. "At nine-fifteen, I call the guard and give him my work slip for nine-thirty. I tell him I forgot I was on the shift, but I can still make it if I hustle. Once we get outside on our way to the laundry plant, I fake getting sick and let him get me to the infirmary."

"Yeah, good," Lorre nodded. "Meanwhile, I'll be going through my own sick routine and hopefully I'll be there when you arrive. If not, wait for me."

"Don't worry, I'm not stupid, you know. I'll let

them get *me* on into the emergency room. You just make sure you get to the same place!"

"I'll get there. And Hernandez will be ready, too."

"After that, it's simple," Jack added. "We just take the guard and use the ambulance for our getaway."

Lorre chewed his bottom lip slightly, then tugged at the corner of his dark mustache. "Yeah, it's a real snap—on paper. Let's hope it goes down that smooth." He took a deep breath to stop the butterflies, then nodded at the guard. "Okay, we better break it up before old Frog-eyes gets suspicious. Nine-thirty!" He stared straight at his friend with a look signifying luck, then spun away to jog a lap around the yard. Jack sauntered slowly back toward the steam house.

Lorre Clauson looked somewhat sinister to people who didn't know him. Dark hair and eyes gave him an even more menacing look, and the drooping mustache made him look like a spy from one of those third-rate foreign movies he had seen in the past. He jerked his head back as he jogged, rippling the muscles in his powerful neck and back. An exhilarating surge ran through his large body: running was pure enjoyment.

He had been a good athlete in his high school days, and a college scholarship lay ahead. Then there had been the car wreck, his banged-up knee, and broken arm, and the scholarship had gone down the drain. He had tried the college route anyway, hoping to work his way through and build his knee back to full strength. But it hadn't worked. He found the studies too tough and dropped out to work for a shipping firm in his home town.

Then came *that* night . . . just like that, all his dreams and hopes were gone. And now he was here on a twenty-year, third-degree murder sentence, with parole possible after serving ten. But three years had given him his fill, and now he was going to try breaking out in order to keep his sanity.

The plan had been set for several months. Initially, it had just been he and Jack, but they soon realized they would need help. Finally, they added Bill Hernandez. An infirmary worker, Hernandez had gotten on friendly terms with several of the ambulance drivers, and almost nightly he stopped to chat with whichever one was on duty. Tonight that friendliness would hopefully pay off.

Lorre's partners were in for big sentences. Hernandez had a twenty-five year term for four counts of armed robbery, second conviction. Schumacher was in for life for the shooting death of a drug store owner. He had already served two years when Lorre met him, and, from his acquaintanceship, Lorre still couldn't believe Jack had shot and killed a man. Schumacher had told him he had been shooting up speed the night of the killing or he wouldn't have even considered pulling the trigger. Lorre believed him. As far as he was concerned, Jack was a quiet, nice guy, too nice to ever be a killer.

Lorre puffed to a walk and began one more turn around the yard. Night was coming on, the already gray sky turning a murky red-brown. The Midwest was the only place in the world where it got that

10

color that time of the year, he had once been told by a college friend. He stared at it again, watching the clouds rolling, building and powerful, then decided it must be true.

"What d'ya think, Clauson? We in for some snow?" The guard smiled down off the watch turret as he shouted the question.

Lorre paused and smiled back. Joe Coleman was the one guard in this place he could stand. The others were so high and mighty. They'd never take a minute to talk like Joe. "God, sure hope not!" he shouted back. "If it does, you'll freeze your butt off up there."

"Aw, hell, I'll survive," Coleman responded. "Once the cold sets in, you clowns never want to stick your noses out anyway, so I'll be able to sit back and keep warm. As a matter of fact, if I were you, I'd get inside. That damn wind is getting a mite chilly." He stepped back into the turret shelter, waving as he did so.

Lorre waved back, then continued on toward the square, drab building that comprised his cellblock area. The whistles sounded, signaling the end of recreation and the start of assembly for the evening meal. Lorre jogged the final forty yards to get near the front of the line. He wanted through early so he'd have plenty of time to prepare for his part in the escape. He got fifth in line, then growled at the guys behind him to quit shoving. The guards also began getting the line in order as the convicts stood waiting for the doors to the mess hall to open.

It was the guard they called "Frog eyes" who finally opened the door to admit the first ten men. The mess hall had its usual cold, gray look. About as welcome as a stone wall, Lorre thought, as he picked up his tray and spoon. The plastic dishes clattered as another prisoner pushed a stack toward the line of men.

Lorre peered ahead at the evening's fare, noting with some satisfaction that liver was being served. Most of the cons hated liver, but it had always been one of his favorites. Good omen, he thought, my favorite food to prepare for the move. "Pile it on, Hank," he smiled at the man on the KP line as he came up to the liver, "this is the food of the gods!"

Hank grimaced as he forked over two slabs. "Geez, I think the slop we used to give our hogs was better than this. How the hell you can eat it is beyond me!"

Lorre just smiled in response and moved on through the line. Although he knew many of the prisoners, he rarely associated with them. He had the tag of a loner, and his six-foot-three, 220-pound frame combined with his looks kept the others at a distance. He sat quietly by himself, wolfing down the food with satisfaction.

"Hey, Allmon!" He gestured to Frog-eyes as he called across the room. The guard moved slowly over to respond. "Hey. Okay if I head back to my cell? Like to write a few letters tonight before lights out."

"Well, I dunno. We shouldn't go bending the rules just because you've got an itch for the pen," Frog-eyes laughed at his own pun then scratched the back of his neck, causing his pop eyes to protrude even further.

Lorre looked back at his nearly empty tray to avoid looking at the guard's eyes.

"Aw, hell, why not?" the guard shrugged. "I guess it's okay. You ready now?"

Lorre gulped the last of his potato and grabbed the half slice of remaining bread. "Yeah, let's go." He picked up his tray and deposited it at the clean-up point, nodding briefly to another con working the garbage line. Then he made his way to the exit and waited while Allmon opened the gate. "Thanks," he nodded as he said it, then turned down the empty hall toward where another guard stood by the second exit door. "Thanks a lot."

The second exit was also unbarred following a wave from Allmon, and Lorre moved outside past the lines of waiting prisoners. A third guard moved to intercept him and he stopped and waited. "Got permission from Allmon to head back to my cell early," he said to the approaching guard. "I got a few letters to knock out tonight if it's okay."

The man looked him over slowly, then motioned with his shotgun to keep moving. Lorre waved and continued on, stopping again and waiting silently for yet another guard to open his cellblock door.

"Missing ol' home sweet home, huh?" the guard chuckled. "Well, come on, little fella, we'll get you all tucked in."

Lorre glowered. He had grown to hate this man for his big mouth. They walked forward toward the interior cell row, the outer gate clanging behind them. The guard stood back until Lorre stepped to one side, then he unlocked the second door. Lorre walked by and on toward his cell. The guard watched till he entered, then pressed a button to lock the cell door. Lorre listened to the click, then settled into the chair by his small writing desk, pulled out several sheets of paper, and pretended to write. The guard stared over the cell row for a few more seconds, then turned and walked back to the outer door.

Lorre checked his watch. Seven-fifteen. Less than two hours to get ready for his part of the plan. He kept on his light work jacket. He'd need it later. Right now it was chilly enough that the guard wouldn't think anything unusual about him still wearing it. His hands felt clammy and his stomach was churning. Can't let this get me upset, he thought. Maybe the best bet would be to get some rest. He'd never be able to sleep, but at least lying back might help him relax.

Christ, some nerve! he thought again as he lay back on the bunk. What if everything didn't go smoothly? What if he couldn't convince the guard to take him to the infirmary? Or what if they couldn't overpower the guard once there? Too many "ifs" in this operation to give him a sense of security. But Jesus! He just had to take this chance. If he got shot or recaptured, at least he would have tried! And what the hell, all they could do is add on years if he was retaken. Twenty-five or thirty wouldn't be any worse than twenty for parole once it got up that high.

14

The thoughts crowded around him as he tried to sort out all the complications. Small beads of perspiration rose on his forehead. He shook his head and thought about home. He probably missed that more than anything. He needed to get home.

He thought back to the time he and his father had gone goose hunting on an evening just like tonight. They had walked several miles along the edge of a marsh, approaching an area his father knew to be a good feeding ground for the big Canadian honkers. It was nearly dusk and the wind was picking up.

"Well, we should be on top of a flock any second now," his father winked as he whispered hoarsely to his gangly seventeen-year-old son. "Now remember, lead them good and don't let them get up too high or they'll just shake off the shot with those heavy feathers. Ready?"

Lorre nodded excitedly and they moved together over a small knoll. The first sight was unbelievable.

For nearly a mile in front of them, the marsh was filled with birds—everything from teal and mud hens to the huge Canadians his father had brought him here to bag. Directly in front of them a group of six geese rose up at the sight of the two men. Both Lorre and his father swung their guns into position.

"Take the lead one, son!" his father shouted even though the air was fairly quiet. "I'll get the one in the rear."

Lorre followed the goose carefully, leading a little, then a little more. It was an ideal shot and he knew he couldn't miss. He had less than fifty yards to shoot. But as he aimed he saw the wings of the big bird strain into the air, pulling the graceful body along. His finger froze at the trigger as he watched the combination of power and grace in action.

At his shoulder he heard his father's gun explode, then he noticed the back bird fall. He regained his sight on the leader but still could not fire. Finally, he lowered the gun.

"Come on." He felt his father's arm around his shoulders. "We'll get mine and go home. It's more than enough for a meal."

Lorre stopped and looked at his father. "Thanks, Dad."

Lorre sat up with a start, glancing at his watch. Eight-forty. He must have dozed. He hadn't even heard the other prisoners coming in, but now he could see them resting or working in their own cells. He looked down the row. A new guard was on, one he hadn't seen before. Well, maybe all the better; a new guard might want to try harder to make sure the shift went okay. The butterflies returned as Lorre realized he was rationalizing.

He stood up, trying to calm himself down. Twisting his face into a contortion of pain, he leaned through the bars and shouted. "Guard! Guard! Help me! Help!" Then he sank down to his knees, holding his stomach.

The guard glanced down the row at the noise, saw Lorre on his knees with one arm through the bars, and quickly opened the door, rushing along the row till he reached the cell. "What's the matter? You sick or something?"

Lorre nodded weakly, still holding his stomach. "It's my gut. The pain is killing me. I . . ." he paused and coughed, "I've gotta see a doctor, it hurts!" He stopped and coughed again then moaned loudly.

"Okay, okay! Come on, get back from the door some so I can get it open." The guard pushed Lorre's arm back through the bars. "Just hold in there while I call for some help!" He raced back to the emergency phone and shouted something quickly into the receiver.

Rushing back, he unlocked the door and helped Lorre off the floor onto the chair by his desk. Then he yelled back over his shoulder as the sound of footsteps echoed off the corridor walls.

"Hey! Bring that stretcher in here. It's in the closet there, on your left. And hurry up, willya, this guy's bad sick!"

The new guard made his way noisily down the hall as prisoners lined up at their doors to watch the unexpected entertainment. Ignoring them, he yanked the door all the way open and slid the stretcher inside, where the first guard helped roll it open. Taking Lorre's arm, he helped him down onto the cot. A third guard appeared at the cell door, but made no effort to help. "Take the foot!" The first guard picked up the stretcher at Lorre's head and the second grabbed the other end at the command.

They moved rapidly down the hall, stopping outside the corridor entrance while the first guard passed brief instructions to the third. Then they rushed on toward the cellblock's outer gate. Once outside, they turned quickly toward the infirmary while Lorre again moaned loudly. The shock of the now icy air nearly took Lorre's breath away. The wind was also gusting harder.

"Hurry up," gasped the first guard. "Let's get him out of this cold before he gets worse."

The second nodded and picked up the pace. At the infirmary door, a prisoner aide held the doors wide, while another took the stretcher from the second guard. He turned back toward the cellblock, motioning the first to stay with the stretcher. A civilian orderly wheeled in a rolling cot to help transport the sick prisoner. Lorre checked his watch. Nine-ten. He moaned again.

"Let's get him down to emergency," the orderly said calmly. "It could be appendicitis." The guard nodded and helped roll the cot down the hall. It was nearly deserted except for a nurse or orderly here and there. They swung the cot into the emergency room. Lorre took in the entire room as they entered, noting Hernandez near the exit. The look telegraphed between them in that split second was all Lorre needed to know everything was still go.

Now the cot was stopped and Lorre looked around the room. Small, and nearly empty. Besides Hernandez, his guard, and the orderly, only a nurse was there, and she was on the phone to the local hospital. Putting down the phone, she said crisply to the orderly, "Okay, let's get his pressure and pulse before loading."

The orderly reached for the bag beside him, but before he could complete the move, the hallway

18

erupted with more noise and the door swung open as another cot, carrying Jack Schumacher, rolled into the room. The nurse looked inquiringly at the orderly in the lead.

"I don't know," he shrugged. "Maybe food poisoning or something. His complaints sound like the symptoms."

Lorre's guard stepped back to the doorway and spoke to a new guard accompanying Schumacher. The first orderly continued to work on charting Lorre's blood pressure, while the nurse went back to the phone to alert of the newest case.

The second guard said a couple of words, then left. Hernandez watched cautiously, then stepped out and motioned to the ambulance driver, who began backing his vehicle into the loading zone.

"Should we take them both on this one?" Hernandez asked. "Or you want me to get Frank's rig back in here, too?"

"You know the rules," the nurse said, putting down the phone. "One prisoner per ambulance with a guard accompanying. What's his BP?" The question was directed to the orderly at Lorre's arm.

"Well, it's normal, I think." He looked puzzled. "But that doesn't make sense, does it? Better check it once more."

Lorre decided it was time to make a move. Moaning loudly, he clutched again at his stomach and began thrashing wildly. "My God, my God!" he shouted. "Somebody help me! It hurts!"

The guard stepped across from the door to help control Lorre's thrashing, while the orderly began moving around the other side. But as the orderly reached Lorre's feet, Lorre lashed out to kick the man squarely in the stomach. He doubled in pain, falling to the floor. Almost simultaneously, Lorre swung at the surprised guard, hitting him squarely in the face. The force of the blow knocked him down, directly in front of Hernandez.

The second guard rushed through door at the noise, drawing his gun and aiming it at Lorre. Schumacher was on his feet like a cat, and locking his hands, he brought them down like a club on the back of the guard's neck. The man crumpled to the floor and lay still. "Get his gun!" Lorre ordered, and Schumacher retrieved it.

The first guard started to get up, but Hernandez pulled one of the doctor's bags from a shelf and brought it down on his head. The guard sank back to the floor. Hernandez grabbed the guard's gun, motioning the orderlies and nurse to the opposite corner. "Quiet," he hissed, "or you're dead!"

None of them moved or spoke. Jack jumped to the door and looked down the hall. There was no further activity. Bolting the door, he turned back, glancing around the room. "Here," he said, grabbing some tape and tossing it to the orderly who had accompanied his cot. "Lace them up. Quick!" He motioned to the other two, then moved to the phone and pulled the receiver loose, tossing it into the wastebasket. The orderly began wrapping the nurse's and other orderly's hands together.

"Okay, Bill, let's see how well you've made up to that ambulance man." Lorre nodded at the door as he spoke in a tense whisper.

Hernandez tossed him the gun, then stepped outside. He blinked back tears as the icy wind hit him full in the face. "Hey, Jimmie, the nurse is about ready to send this one in. Get your back door open, willya?" He rubbed his hands and turned up his coat collar while waiting for the driver to come around to the rear of the ambulance. "Hey, then couldya give us a hand in here? This one's a biggie!"

The driver nodded, then propped open the doors and came up the steps to Hernandez' side. "Christ, it's cold out here," he said, "bet we'll see some snow by morning. Or at least by tomorrow night. What do you think, Bill? You sure are quiet toni—" he stopped in mid-sentence as he stepped into the room to face the gun in Lorre's hand.

Lorre motioned him over to the orderly, who had finished binding the nurse and his co-worker. "Get him tied up too," he ordered, "and snap it up unless you want a busted head."

The orderly hurriedly began the binding while Schumacher stuffed gauze into the others' mouths. Lorre turned back to Hernandez. "Okay, Bill, get that driver's coat and wallet. You sure you know the password at the gate?"

"Yeah, I heard it lots of times," Bill answered as he slipped off his coat and took the driver's. "It's Gray. Those clowns think they're really being sly, but anybody here knows that code by now." He glanced at the driver, whose eyes glinted darkly at the man he had befriended.

Schumacher stuffed some gauze in the driver's

mouth, then motioned the other man to turn around.

"All right, tie him up and let's get going," Lorre said, "before someone gets on to us."

"Tie him up, hell," Schumacher answered, "I got faster plans." Swinging the gun back, he crashed it down on the orderly's head. The man crumpled to the floor and blood welled up where the gun barrel had struck.

"What the hell are you doing?" Lorre leaped toward the downed man. "We said no one gets hurt and then you do an idiot thing like that. Christ, man, you coulda killed him with a shot like that!"

Schumacher shrugged and smiled slightly. "We can waste all night here, man," he answered. "I'm just saving us some time. Now let's get going."

Lorre glared at him, then motioned to Hernandez. "All right, then, let's do it."

They stepped out into the cold. Lorre climbed in back while Jack took the orderly's spot in the cab. Hernandez slipped in behind the wheel. Lorre pulled the doors shut, then moved to the front, where Hernandez pulled open the vent between the cab and the rear.

"Okay, nice and easy, just like you've seen the pros do it," Lorre said quietly.

Bill started the ambulance and moved it forward. Security was double and the ambulance had to pass through two checks. A guard waved them to a stop and Bill complied.

"Password?" he asked, holding his shotgun loosely over his arm.

"Gray—just like tonight, huh?" Hernandez smiled.

"That's just fine," the guard responded. "Sure don't envy you on the road tonight. That damn wind just about blows you off the side." He waved the ambulance on.

They passed through the first gate, then across a hundred-yard stretch between the main wall and a barbed-wire enclosure. A second guard stepped from a small shack, signaling for the ambulance to stop. Bill slowed it, then halted alongside the shack. "What you got there?" the smiling guard asked, waving the gun at the rear of the vehicle. "Anything important tonight?"

"Think it's an appendicitis," Hernandez answered. "He's sure a big one."

"Well, better get it on the road, then. What's the pass?"

"Gray."

"Okay. Have a good trip." The guard walked over and started to pull the gate aside.

"Say, just a second. I just noticed something here!" he yelled, pointing to the rear of the ambulance. "Come on back here, willya?"

Bill looked quickly at Schumacher who looked to Lorre. Lorre nodded, then turned to face the rear door. Hernandez climbed out slowly and walked along the side toward the guard. Schumacher quickly slipped out the other door before Lorre could stop him.

"Damn fool," Lorre hissed under his breath, "he'll get us all killed!"

"Now see here," the guard pointed to the rear lights. "This bulb's about to go, and so is that one there on the door. And look at this," he grabbed the door handle and Bill flinched, "this ain't even properly hooked. Want to lose your cargo?" He grinned at Bill and unhooked the door to reseal it.

The grin froze on his face then turned to a look of disbelief as the shot stopped his movement. He appeared glued to the door for a split second before the sound of the gun seemed to penetrate Bill's ears. The guard clawed at the door then slumped to the ground as Jack stepped away from the ambulance's edge.

Lorre pushed the door open, saw the guard lying on the ground and the shocked look on Bill's face. Then he whirled to face Schumacher. "What the hell are you doing? Why this?"

"He was going to open the door. He'd have seen you." Jack's voice and face seemed unconcerned as he glanced down at the guard. "Couldn't let that happen now, could I?"

"He wouldn't have looked in here. I heard him. He was just going to reseal the door. You fool!" He spat the words at him and Jack's face flashed briefly with anger, illuminated suddenly by a spotlight turned their way. The guards on the wall had heard the shot and now they were checking.

"Quick, get the gate!" Lorre shouted to Bill, pulling the door shut again as he sat back into the ambulance. Hernandez ran for the gate, while Jack slid in behind the wheel. Lorre could hear shots, then saw the dirt kick up around Hernandez in front of

24

them. "Kill those headlights, you idiot," he shouted at Jack. "You're setting him up like he's in a shooting gallery!"

Schumacher slapped off the lights as Hernandez finished pulling the gate aside and ran for the passenger door. He jerked open the door and all three heard bullets thump into the ambulance walls.

Bill looked stunned for a second, then tried to climb into the cab. Instead, he coughed slightly, grabbed at his left side and fell to the ground. Lorre started to push at the back door to get out and help him, but before he could move, the ambulance jumped forward and picked up speed, throwing him off balance. The back door swung open and he saw Hernandez slump face forward on the road as the spotlights circled him.

Then they were gone, lost to the lights in the quickly-blackening countryside. Lorre turned back to the front of the ambulance, slamming the door behind him. Schumacher reached across to latch the passenger door, then he stepped down on the footfeed and the ambulance jumped ahead again. Lorre sat back on the transport cot shaking his head numbly. In the cab, he heard Jack begin to whistle, almost gaily.

CHAPTER TWO

Rollie and Jean Patterson had first thought of moving to the country just after their marriage, but a combination of school, jobs, and then the availability of a reasonably priced home, with a few acres of land surrounding it, had held them back. Finally, after Rollie's permanent assignment to the Hollysberg department, they had found what they were looking for and taken the step.

The home was nothing special, simply an older farmhouse with a barn and two outer sheds. A huge grove of cottonwood trees took up one of the five acres. The rest had been lush grassland, now turned brown as winter approached. They had spent the late summer months and early fall getting the house reinsulated, and the latest addition had been a new electric furnace that could be switched to an emergency fuel oil supply, in case of power failure.

Now the young couple felt both secure and happy in their new surroundings. They were especially looking forward to the upcoming year. Their first baby was only a month away, Rollie was due for a big raise, and they were hoping to buy some small farm animals, like a pony, to add on as sort of a hobby. Life, they felt, was being particularly good.

Rollie was up late this November evening, and Jean, unable to sleep because of the baby's kicking, climbed out of bed to join him for some coffee. They heard the rain start and Rollie walked outside to see if it was sleeting. Jean felt the cold air roll in as the door opened and closed with his leaving and returning. He rubbed his hands as he walked to the table.

"Boy, it's bitter out there!" he exclaimed, blowing on his hands and then reaching out to touch his wife on the neck. He laughed as she screamed and jumped back out of his way. She shivered and stepped in front of a heating vent. He joined her and rubbed his hands in front of the flow of warm air.

"God, I hate to think of work out there tomorrow. It'll be nothing but cars in the ditch or stalled motorists all day. Ah, the rough life of a cop." He laughed again as he put his arm around Jean, and she added a chuckle.

"You love it and you know it," she said, smiling at her still-tanned husband. "And I love you!" She kissed him lightly, then made her way heavily to the table, where she sat down and poured herself another cup of coffee.

She stared across the table at her husband. Rollie was the "perfect" highway patrolman. Just like the brochures liked to list them. He was lean and nearly six-foot-one. She always felt like a shrimp next to him, being a full seven inches shorter. People were always teasing them about looking like Mutt and Jeff, even though they looked somewhat alike with their brown hair and eyes. Teasing remarks like that always brought out Jean's devilish grin, which people said enhanced her pixieish beauty.

Right now, however, she felt anything but pixieish. She was tired and looked it. Carrying the baby was taking its toll on her petite frame. "You know, for once, I wish I could sleep at night," Jean said as Rollie smiled across at her. "I'll really be glad when *he's* finally out of there." She nodded to her bulging stomach.

"Yeah, I know," Rollie sighed in agreement. "The time'll come soon enough though, so hang in there." He reached over and patted her stomach in reassurance and she gave him a weak grin.

Jean had been a teacher up through the past spring. When she found out she was pregnant, she decided to prepare for the baby instead of continuing her career for one more semester. Rollie was right, she thought now. The baby would be coming soon enough. But she really was exhausted.

"Why not turn on the radio so we can hear the weather?" she asked. "The wind sounds bad." Rollie nodded and flicked on the switch. They sipped their coffee together, not talking, till the forecast came on.

"It looks like winter is finally here." The tired announcer tried to sound as cheery as possible while wrapping up his midnight shift. "With a low-pressure system that's moved in from the north, combined with a moisture-filled flow of warm air from the southwest, we can look for increased rain turning to snow as the day continues. The amount of snow will depend on how long our temperatures stay above freezing, although early indications are they'll be dropping rapidly over the next four or five hours. We could see below-zero temperatures by tomorrow night."

He continued in his best folksy style: "So, if you're going outdoors much tomorrow, I'd recommend bundling up good and planning on an early start home from work to avoid bad traffic conditions. Well, we'll be right back with a summary of the news and some more on that big prison break at Mammoth Falls after this important word from Sunco."

Jean glanced quickly to her husband with a questioning look, but he just shrugged and absently rubbed his hands together once more. He sipped his coffee again as they waited for the announcer's return.

"At the top of the news this hour is the prison break from the State Penitentiary at Mammoth Falls," the announcer said. "In a daring move, two maximum-security convicts escaped tonight in a city ambulance. A third prisoner, William Hernandez, thirty-three, and a guard, John Schubeck, thirty, were killed in gunfire surrounding the escape. A third man, Paul Fisher, an orderly in the prison infirmary, is in critical condition from a blow to his head. Two guards, injured in the escape, have been treated and released.

"The two prisoners who escaped using the city ambulance are twenty-five-year-old Lorre Clauson and twenty-eight-year-old Jack Schumacher. Clauson has dark hair and eyes, a dark mustache and is six-foot-three, 220 pounds. Schumacher is five-ten, 180 pounds, with blond hair, blue eyes, and a blond mustache. The men were believed to be headed west, although police have been unable to locate the ambulance. Both men are armed and considered dangerous. The escape seems to have. . . ."

Rollie reached over and snapped off the radio, rubbing his chin as he leaned back.

"Rollie, I'm scared. If they're headed west, they could be in this area. What happens if you come across them?" Jean reached across the table and grabbed one of her husband's hands in both of hers. "Do you think you'll have to join in the search?"

Rollie nodded, then smiled. "Now don't worry. If we do find them, we're not stupid enough to go charging in like rookies. We'll have plenty of help wherever we are, and we probably won't even have to fire a shot. Those men are going to have to get rid of that ambulance, and when they do, they'll be on foot. It's too cold and wet out there for them to wander around for very long. In the meantime, we'll be warm, dry, and ready for them." He smiled again and kissed one of her hands. "I think I know enough about police work to take care of myself. Okay?"

Jean relaxed a little at his reassuring tone of voice. She knew he did indeed know how to take care of himself. He'd only been a patrolman for three years, but his record was distinguished. Following a head-of-the-class finish in the academy, he'd notched an impressive service record, including a state patrol citation, and now he'd been able to pick his own job site because of it. That's why they'd come to Hollysberg in the first place. It was a plum position if you liked quiet, out-of-the-way places, and it was high on the list of many of the officers. Rollie had jumped at his chance to get it on a five-year assignment. Permanent duty in the state highway patrol didn't come easy.

He'd proven himself as a good cop, and Jean knew his reputation. "Well, all I can say is I'm glad you're on my side. I sure wouldn't want to be any ol' escaped prisoner trying to stay out of your way."

Rollie leaned over the table and kissed her, then got up and walked to the bedroom. "Hey, I've got to get some sleep. My shift is at six and it'll be a forty-five-minute drive to the station in this weather. What d'ya say?"

She nodded sleepily, knowing that probably sleep still wouldn't come, despite her tired feeling.

"If this snow gets any heavier, I'll try to give you a call later in the day to make sure everything's all right!" Rollie shouted from the kitchen where he'd been banging around for about fifteen minutes.

Jean nodded groggily in her half sleep, knowing in her mind she was giving him a complete answer.

"And if the electricity goes off, just flip the switch by the thermostat to get the oil heat started, then

I'll get it back over when I get home." He walked back into the bedroom, lowering his voice and snapping his heavy insulated patrolman's coat as he walked. "But I doubt you'll have any problems anyway."

Jean was still in the same position he'd left her when he climbed from the bed. He smiled and bent over to kiss her on the cheek.

"Okay?"

"Umm-hmm," she smiled without opening her eyes. He caressed her softly on the shoulder, then turned and walked to the kitchen door.

"Rollie."

He looked back.

"Be careful."

"I will . . . promise." He stepped out into the cold.

Jean shivered involuntarily, then again, as she thought of the cold air, snuggled down deeper beneath the blankets. She'd get up soon, she promised herself; just as soon as she caught up on a little of her sleep. She yawned and wrapped both arms around her stomach. There was still plenty of time for the day to begin.

The briefing room was crowded and steaming from the moisture off the men's clothes, now vaporizing in the warm air. It reminded Rollie of his old high school locker room following a football game on a cold night, only here there was no shower noise, just the buzz of voices.

"All right, all right, let's do it, okay?" Sergeant Granzetti's deep bass boomed out over the room, automatically lowering the buzz. He stared at the men, waiting for them to get into some semblance of order, then rustled through the papers in his hands.

"Okay, as you all know by now, we've called on both Watches One and Two for this shift due to the expected pile-up of activity due to the storm. Watch One will be on patrol as assigned and you members of Two will be kept here in the city to answer in-town calls and clear up any traffic problems. Any questions on that?" His eyes darted from one small group of men to another as if daring someone to speak. No one did.

"Good! Now, besides the storm, which you all smell like you've found out about. . . ." He paused as the patrolmen broke into laughter. "Besides the storm, we've got the breakout, and the lieutenant will fill you in." He looked toward a slender, mustachioed man, lounging as if half asleep in a chair behind him. The lieutenant did not stand, but rather took a sheet handed him by the sergeant and began droning out the report on the prison break.

Rollie sat back with a disgusted look as he listened to the unconcerned voice reading things he'd already heard on his home and car radios. He didn't like the lieutenant and now he painted a mental picture of how *he* would present similar material once he achieved that rank. The favorable impression of himself up there cheered him and he sat up straighter in his chair.

"Well, that's all we have from central as of now. The possibility of them getting into our sector is slight, but in case, well. . . ." The lieutenant let the sentence dangle to let his men put in their own endings.

"The primary thing is helping people through this storm and answering emergencies," he continued. "If any of you do come in contact with these convicts, I want an immediate call into headquarters for a back-up. Is that understood?"

The patrolmen agreed, as the lieutenant seemed to open his eyes fully for the first time. Looking satisfied, he nodded back to his sergeant.

"All right, now," Granzetti began, "we're extending both watches for an additional four hours, and. . . ." He stopped as the room filled with groans, "*And,* if the need requires, you'll be on even longer to assist Watch Three." More groans. "Now here's some of the things that came down last night on Three." He continued reading through the sheets for several minutes as Rollie and his partner, Mike Henson, jotted things rapidly onto their pocket notepads.

The Hollysberg Patrol Center ran on a three-watch rotation with twelve patrolmen out on each watch. The six cars were dispersed over a wide area and Rollie and Mike would be expected roughly to cover a 100-square-mile sector. Although Hollysberg itself was a fair-size community, the surrounding countryside was bleak, with farms and ranches scattered few and far between. Only two other towns of any size were within the region. The locale allowed for a leisurely pace on most days, but when storms rolled in, as Rollie was discovering, it caused a major hassle.

34

Granzetti finished reading a list of license-plate numbers and descriptions of stolen vehicles which might turn up in the area, then tossed his handful of papers on a small desk beside him. "Okay, it's going to be rough today, so keep your heads. We may not be able to get a back-up car to help you, so don't take any chances. Another thing. . . ." He turned back to face the men as they stood to go. "We'll be patched into the hospital and the highway department. If the hospital needs your help, they get it. And if you need a plow to get through, *you* got it. Okay?"

He turned his back to the patrolmen to signify he was finished and Rollie stood and stretched. His pantlegs, wet earlier from the slush on the streets, had nearly dried.

"Coffee first?" Mike said the words almost pleadingly and Rollie laughed and nodded. They made their way to the big pot near the dispatcher's desk, pulled away two steaming cups, and moved into the waiting room to look over their area chart for the day.

"Phew," Rollie whistled as he eyed the map. "Looks like nothin' but good times, huh?"

"Yeah," Mike answered, wincing as he scalded the roof of his mouth. "Jesus Christ! Why do I always do that?" He held his hand over his mouth as if that was going to help the scald.

"Yeah, it'll be tough, no doubt about it," he said, looking at the map. "You know, we've only got one paved road going each way. Let's hope those people out there are going to sit tight."

They stood together, Rollie putting his cup aside

and Mike still clasping his. They stepped out into the still-dark morning. The streets were slushy, but it was getting colder, and Rollie knew the slush would soon become chunks of ice. The snow, too, seemed to have picked up in the half hour since he'd arrived at the station. The wind was howling.

"You have any trouble getting in?" Mike shouted as they trudged toward the patrol car.

"A little," Rollie shouted back, "but I'm more concerned about getting back out tonight!"

Mike nodded agreement, then stopped and drank some more of the coffee as the wind nearly blew the cup from his hand.

Rollie slid into the patrol car's passenger side, checked the shotgun snapped in below the dash to be sure it was secured, then began marking off their safety check list as Mike fought with the driver's side door and finally got inside. "Okay?" He gasped the question, then slurped at his coffee again, eyeing it proudly because he had made it to the car without spilling any.

"Yeah, fine," Rollie answered. "You ready to drive?"

Mike turned a thumb up in answer and turned over the key in the ignition.

Rollie snapped on the police radio, picked up the mike, and reported in.

"Okay, One-Zebra-Nine, you are on Sector G. Is that confirmed?" The dispatcher's voice came across in her usual monotone.

"Ten-four," Rollie answered, replacing the mike.

The radio crackled again. "Update on the escaped

prisoners from Mammoth Falls. . . ." Mike held up on shifting, waiting for the report.

"State headquarters indicates search is being conducted in vicinity of Mule Ridge where last believed ambulance used in the escape was sighted. Will advise as earliest updates arrive."

Rollie and Mike exchanged grins.

"Well, at least we won't have to worry about them. Mule Ridge is way north of our zone," Mike said.

Rollie nodded agreement.

"Now all we have to do is handle the normal, mundane emergencies," Mike added.

"You got it," Rollie answered, settling back and loosening his heavy coat.

Mike gulped the last of his coffee, tossed the styrofoam cup on the floor, then wheeled the car out of the lot.

CHAPTER THREE

The ambulance had been bumping along a dirt road for nearly an hour when Jack finally pulled off and stopped the engine. It had been more than two hours since they had sped away from the prison gate, and now they were alone, surrounded by the trees and the night.

Lorre climbed down from the back and stared at his companion. Ignoring him, Jack stretched heavily and yawned. They had not spoken.

Lorre fingered the guard's revolver, which had not left his hand since the escape. Now he slipped it into his belt as he walked to Jack's side. The wind pushed him along. He could feel the storm approaching. "Well?" He looked Jack squarely in the face, fighting off the urge to shiver.

"Well, what?" Jack replied, staring back at him and blowing on his hands. He stepped more into the shelter of the ambulance as the wind gusted higher.

"What the hell was *that* all about back there?"

"I don't know what you mean," Jack answered as if dismissing the conversation. "I think I acted the same as always."

"The same as always!" Lorre exploded, stepping up beside him. "When the hell have you *always* acted like a cold-blooded killer!" He turned and kicked the ambulance tire in disgust. "Christ, you really screwed it by killing that guard! If you hadn't been so quick on the trigger, maybe even by now they wouldn't have known about the escape going down—at least for an hour. At least!" He jabbed a finger in Schumacher's face to emphasize his point.

"Well, what did you expect me to do?" Jack whined, "Let him open that door and see you?"

"See me? Shit!" Lorre shook his head. "The man was going to secure the door. And besides, why not just bang him on the head? You seem to be real good at that, *too*. What a bunch of bullshit! All you accomplished was a giveaway on our move; a dead guard, Bill dead—or at least hurt bad! See *me*!" He wheeled at the tire again but held up kicking it a second time. "And that's another thing. Why didn't you give me time to get Bill back into the cab?"

"Because we didn't have time, man," Schumacher whined again. "Those other guards would have been on us by the time you got all that done. I *had* to go when I did." He looked up and down the road as if maybe they should end the conversation and start moving again.

Lorre banged his hand against the ambulance

wall, cursing to himself. Then he walked back to the rear end and slammed the door. "Well, one thing's sure. We've got to ditch this thing soon because every cop in the state has gotta be looking for it. How much gas we got left?"

Lorre turned back to Schumacher as he asked the question and noticed how unconcerned his partner seemed about what had transpired. He had always thought his friend to be the easygoing, nice-guy type. Too nice to ever knowingly have killed. Now? Well, he had committed himself to this mess and he'd stick it out, but at the earliest possible, he'd make sure they parted paths.

Schumacher walked over to the cab and switched on the key. He gasped, jerking his head out, with a panicky look on his face. "Good God, we're almost empty! How in hell can that be?" He looked at Lorre. "Hernandez said these things are *always* filled before the night shift!"

"Let me see that," Lorre shoved him aside and stared at the gauge. The needle was right above the empty line. As he watched it, the needle wavered and seemed to drop some more. "Pull this thing ahead!" he ordered, standing back from the door.

"What?" Schumacher looked at him with surprise.

"I said pull it ahead—a few feet."

Schumacher shrugged and stepped inside, starting the engine and rolling it ahead.

"Okay!" Lorre shouted. He carefully eyed the ground where the vehicle had stood. A small, dark stain broke the otherwise even dullness of the ground. He knelt and pinched at the spot, sniffing his fingers.

"Shit, it's gas! The damn gas tank is leaking! Of all the rotten luck. It's gotta be the one ambulance in the whole fleet with anything wrong, as good as they keep these things running."

"Maybe one of those bullets hit it," Schumacher offered as Lorre stood.

"Yeah. . . ." Lorre half growled the word as he mulled over the possibility. "Nah. If a bullet had hit that thing, it'd either have blown us up or leaked out gas so fast we'd have gone nowhere at all. That leak's too slow."

He paced back and forth. "What difference does it make, anyway? We've got to get back on the road for as long as possible before the gas is completely gone. Maybe try to find some other car or truck or something."

Now he could no longer repress the urge to shiver and did so. "Jeez, it's cold out here. If only that wind would die down."

"Not much luck in finding anything this way," Jack said as they walked to the ambulance and climbed in the cab. "That's why we came this way in the first place, remember? 'Cause there's so few people out here. It was your idea." Jack was on the offensive now and his voice tone rose as he accused. "We've been on this goddamn road for an hour and haven't seen anything that even looks like a building, let alone a house or a car."

Lorre settled in on the passenger side. "Well, maybe we'll get luckier down the road," he grumbled, crossing his arms. He preferred not to talk to Jack at all. He was still fuming about Jack's behavior at the prison. He knew now that both he and Hernandez had been patsies, and Jack would probably fend only for himself if they found themselves in further trouble.

Lorre looked over at his partner, who was focusing his attention on the road and the gas gauge. Jack had always seemed so calm and conservative. Christ, it was only recently that he'd even considered growing the almost-standard mustache so prevalent among the inmates. And now that he had the growth, it was kept neatly trimmed.

Lorre had been attracted to Jack in the first place by his quiet demeanor. He'd never wisecracked or even picked on anyone. They had gotten along well together. Jack never bothered Lorre, never infringed on his privacy. But, he'd been there to talk when Lorre wanted to.

Now, Lorre stared at the man he was riding with as if he were a stranger. It definitely wasn't the Jack Lorre thought he knew so well.

Jack began whistling again, softly at first, then slightly louder. The sound rasped across every nerve end in Lorre's body. "Cut it, willya!" he snapped. Jack glanced at him briefly, then stopped. "Christ! Everything's happened tonight, and you're whistling like it was the first day of spring! Just cut it!"

The ambulance shuddered, then jerked, then began losing speed. Jack shifted and continued to nurse it along. They were nearing a hilltop and he rocked his body as the ambulance continued faltering, trying to force it up and over. The ambulance's engine gave another spurt of power and they made the top, then started down the other side as the motor died. Jack turned off the key and continued steering, veering off into the underbrush as they neared the bottom. Guiding it carefully, he headed it between two trees, where it stopped. Setting the emergency brake, he removed the key slowly before speaking. "Well, now what?"

"I don't know. Give me time to think." Lorre opened his door and stepped out, quickly turning his back as an icy blast of wind hit him. He walked back to the road and stared as far as possible. It was black, and empty, except for the brush and trees on both sides. A stick snapped and he turned to face Jack, who was once again rubbing his hands. "I guess we'll stick with the road for now and see what turns up," Lorre said. "If we can find a farm house, we can get some food and clothes, and maybe some transportation. With the ambulance back in there like that, I doubt anyone'll find it soon. Don't think this road gets much use anyway."

Jack nodded, then walked back to the ambulance and swung open the rear doors. Reaching inside, he pulled out the blankets and medical kit. Then he cut holes in the center of each blanket with a pair of scissors in the kit and tossed one to Lorre.

"What the hell am I supposed to do with this?" Lorre asked. He was getting irritated by Jack's self-assurance.

"Wear it. Like a poncho," Jack said quietly, slipping the blanket in his hands over his head. "Our jackets won't be worth a damn against this wind, and we don't know how long we'll be walking."

Lorre relaxed a little and slipped on the blanket. Jack was right. They might be afoot for hours.

"What time is it?"

Lorre looked at his watch, squinting in the darkness. "Nearly midnight. We got five, maybe six hours before it starts getting light. Better get moving. You have any idea at all where we're at?"

"Well, I turned west from Bonnerville, but this road's been twisting and turning a lot. I'd guess about twenty miles northwest of Bonnerville. There oughta be *some* farm house out around here. And there's a town, too."

"Which one's that?"

"Hollysberg."

Lorre nodded and they turned into the wind and began walking. They had gone only a short distance when a light rain began to fall.

The snow was becoming increasingly heavy by the time Jean pulled herself out of bed around seven-thirty. The temperature had dropped to 30 degrees, she learned as she listened to the local announcer. He noted it was expected to continue dropping throughout the day. The newest forecast called for about eight inches of snow.

Whistling cheerfully, Jean poured herself some fresh coffee, filled a bowl with cornflakes, splashed on some milk, and doused them with several spoonfuls of sugar. She hated cornflakes, and she hated milk, but she'd convinced herself they'd be good for her in the latter part of her pregnancy. Eyeing them warily, she dropped, rather than sat, into a chair by the table and began munching. It was monotonous out here, she thought, but after the baby came it would be better. She wished now that she had a dog, or even a cat to keep her company on days like this one.

From time to time she'd had second thoughts about having a family, especially on days when she longed to be back in the classroom. But then she'd think again of the excitement she and Rollie would share with the baby, and how there was still plenty of time to go back to work, and the feeling would pass. There had already been excitement for them just preparing for the event over the past few months. Getting the new house had been a start, and then there were the prenatal classes. Now, she was in the final stages of getting the baby's room ready, a project planned to resume following breakfast.

She reached across the table for a copy of an advertisement that had come in the mail the day before. As she did, a sudden twinge of pain passed through her stomach. It was gone almost as fast as it came and she shrugged it off and returned to the ad, sipping at her coffee as she read about an upcoming clothing sale in Hollysberg. Finally, tossing it aside, she picked up a copy of the book she'd been reading in her spare time. Soon she was engrossed in the newest chapter, forgetting her determination to get an early start on the day's work in the baby room. Her coffee also went unnoticed, growing cold with neglect as she absorbed the details about one of the lead characters dying in a hospital.

By the time the chapter was completed, she felt depressed. The character had died and she laid the book aside slowly, wiping a tear from her cheek. She sat quietly for a few more minutes, lost in her thoughts and feeling very alone.

Rising and stretching, she held a hand to the small of her back, then walked to the window to watch the snow being blown hard across the yard. It was beginning to pile up and enough had fallen to completely blanket the ground and everything on it. She thought of the old pickup truck sheltered inside the shed and wondered if it would start if needed. Walking to the cupboard by the sink, she took down a key, and turned it over in her hands. Now was the time to find out.

With a burst of newfound energy, she hurried into the bedroom and pulled some clothing from the dresser drawer, discarding her bathrobe and nightgown and quickly dressing. Then she walked to the hall closet and pulled out her heavy winter coat. It fit tightly, but she ignored the discomfort and finished buttoning it to the top, snapping the hood into place. Rummaging through a box on the closet floor, she finally pulled out a pair of wool mittens. "There," she said aloud to herself, patting her arms with her mittened hands.

Another twinge of pain ran through her stomach, and she stopped for just a second. Once again, it was gone almost instantly, so she walked to the door and stepped out. The snow was nearly an inch deep now, and she hoped it wouldn't pile up too much before Rollie's shift ended at two. She'd feel a lot more secure with him back home.

I must make quite a sight, she thought, as she made her way to the shed. Just like an old mother duck waddling around. She laughed to herself as she pictured her face on a duck's body. There was no other way to describe herself though, she thought, the way she was wrapped up against the storm with her belly protruding as if leading her on her way.

The faint outlines of a man's footprints near the big sliding door, which was fastened securely with a chain and padlock, caught her eye as she reached the shed. Rollie must have checked the shed before leaving, she decided. Jean walked to the smaller side door and stepped inside.

The pickup door groaned in protest as she pulled it open. The seat was covered with dust. She brushed it away and slid behind the wheel, her stomach crowding it in the process. Inserting the key in the ignition, she stared at the panel for a few seconds. Now, how did Rollie say this thing started? Pump it twice, then let up. She performed the ceremony and turned the key. The engine growled slowly, then caught and chugged along. She roared the motor twice, then switched it off.

Must be getting colder, better get back inside, she thought and struggled out of the truck. Outside, the wind was picking up and she turned her back as it whipped snow into her face. She pulled the door shut firmly, making sure it was latched. Don't need this place full of snow, she thought, turning and checking it once again.

A gust of wind nearly obliterated her view of the house and she realized the storm wasn't at all bad compared to what it could be if the wind's intenseness increased. It was swirling now, too, and a continuation of that could cause real problems for Rollie, not only on the way home, but today as he went about his work. "Come on," she said, looking at the snow-filled sky, "it's not winter time yet. Come on."

She was answered with another gust which filled her face with stinging snow. She quickly pulled a mittened hand up to her face as a windbreak, then shuffled back toward the house. Pausing on the porch, she stamped her feet to knock off the snow, then brushed her pants to clean them. As she reached for the doorknob, another small pain erupted in her stomach. "Good God, what is this?" she muttered to herself, rubbing a hand over her stomach. The pain quickly subsided again. "Better check the medical book."

She slipped inside, snapped the door lock, and stood still, feeling the house's warmth rush over her as she removed her coat and mittens. Walking into the room they had converted to a den, she began searching through the books for the medical journal they had bought early in the pregnancy. She sank down on her knees and looked through several books on the bottom shelf. "Oh, damn it! Where is that thing?"

She looked around disgustedly, then put a hand

on a nearby end table and pulled herself to her feet. Turning, she walked back through the house and into the bedroom. A thorough search of the closet still did not turn up the book. She sat down on the edge of the bed, breathing heavily. Then she remembered, he'd been looking at it in the kitchen when she'd gotten up to join him at midnight.

Smiling, she walked into the kitchen and spotted the book on the corner of the countertop next to the refrigerator. She flipped the pages over, trying to locate a section she thought might give her an answer to the sudden stomach pains. Finally, she found it and, sticking her tongue between her teeth, she picked up the book with both hands and turned to walk to the table. As she turned, she paused, her brain trying to register something unfamiliar. She looked back to the countertop, then out the kitchen window. Only the crackling of the snow against the glass greeted her, yet something was definitely wrong.

What had caused her to stop? It was something from outside. But what? She stared through the window again. Had she seen something move? Involuntarily, she shivered. Must be my imagination, she thought, turning again toward the table. Maybe it had been a stray tree branch torn loose by the wind, or another bird. Sure, that had to be it. She sighed and eased into the chair at the table's edge and began reading. A scratching sound from the rear of the house, however, caused her to stop. She shivered again, slid the chair back and stood, closing the book in the process. It was probably just a branch blowing up against the house, but this, coupled with her uneasy feeling of a few moments earlier was starting to spook her. She had to check this out to satisfy her own curiosity.

She walked toward the back door and the scratching stopped. Jean paused, listening intently. Nothing. She still stood silently, waiting for further sounds, but the only ones were those of the house as each fresh gust of wind whistled around it. She shook her head, forcing a smile and turned back toward the kitchen. Two sharp clicks, almost like the snapping of a lock bolt, stopped her in midstep. She turned back, wavering between checking the noise and panicking. "Don't be a dummy," she admonished herself, opting for the former.

Walking into the living room and across to the back window, she rubbed a circle clear on the glass and peered out. It was white and nothing more. The wind had sculpted the snow into fine-edged shapes and she studied one appreciatively, started to turn away, then froze.

Directly below the window and partially filled in by the rapidly blowing snow was a clearly visible set of a man's footprints. As she stared toward them, two more sharp clicks came from the direction of the back door.

CHAPTER FOUR

Rollie flung himself at the car door, yanked it open and fell inside. Pulling the door shut behind him, he sat puffing and gasping, peeling off one of his wet gloves and wiping the snow from his reddened face. "I think I froze my goddamn eye," he said calmly, closing his stinging left eye and turning toward Mike. "Christ! It's unreal out there! Just unreal!"

"What about the car?" Henson asked, casting a wary eye at the puddles of water beginning to form on the floor and seat beside Rollie as the patrol car's heater thawed his partner out.

"Empty," Rollie answered, beginning to regain his breath. "Driver must've abandoned it earlier and was picked up by another motorist or something. It's frozen up tight." He exhaled slowly and felt around his frozen left eye, blinking several times as the blurriness began to fade.

"Okay, I'll call it in," Mike answered, pulling the microphone from its hook. "Zebra base, this is One-Zebra-Nine, over."

"Zebra base, go ahead," a voice crackled back on the transmitter.

"We have checked the car, and it appears deserted. We believe the motorist may have been picked up, but we'll proceed eastward to see if he may have tried to walk."

"Ten-four, Zebra-Nine." The radio went silent and Mike snapped the mike back into its slot. "You all right?" He glanced over at Rollie.

"Yeah. Fine," Rollie responded, staring out the window toward the faintly visible form of an abandoned car. He had struggled through about fifty yards of snow to get to the car, which was sitting at a crazy angle off the road and partially into the ditch. Drifts were piling up to more then two feet now and the wind's intensity had increased. The temperature was also down, and Rollie had particularly noticed it on his latest venture outside the patrol car's warmth. "What's the latest?" Rollie asked, turning away from the window.

"The forecast I got says six inches on the ground and a predicted eight to ten more before the day's through. Sounds like we'll soon go below zero too. It's a real first-class blizzard."

Rollie eyed his watch. Just after eight. It seemed like they'd been on the road a lot longer. He leaned back and Mike eased the car forward, starting slowly to avoid slipping, then picking up speed.

They were patrolling a relatively open region, with homes and small towns few and far between, and even though they could call for help if necessary, they didn't need the partol car stuck when the emergencies would be piling up as the storm progressed.

As it had grown lighter, they had answered more and more calls, most for stranded drivers. The ice and snow were creating another hazard, too—downed power lines. As they had proceeded deeper into the rural zone of their patrol, they were finding downed lines which had to be checked then called in before too much damage was done or someone was injured by the whiplashing live wires.

"There's another one," Rollie said, pointing to his right. About 100 yards ahead, barely visible through the blowing snow, they could see a line whipped by the wind. As it lashed its way across a farm fence, it sent up a shower of sparks, instigated by the line's touching the steel fencing.

"Zebra base, this is One-Zebra-Nine, over."

"Zebra base."

"Yes, we have a downed line about eleven miles due east of Barton. The line is live and we request a service truck be dispatched ASAP."

"Ten-four, Zebra-Nine . . . and Zebra-Nine," the voice took on an urgent tone as if cautioning against cutting off the call. "We had a call from the Hollysberg Hospital. A doctor there—Dr. Jonas—reports need of a check on a patient in your zone for possible assistance and transport. The address lists fourteen miles east and three north of Barton. Can you handle?" the dispatcher asked.

"Ten-four."

"Good." The dispatcher sounded relieved, and Rollie noted with interest that it was the first time he'd heard emotion in her voice since he'd come on the Hollysberg force. "The farmer's name there is Schmidt," she added. "I will inform Dr. Jonas of your response."

"Ten-four." Rollie returned the mike to its hook. "That's a gravel side road. What do you think?"

"No sweat, big fella," Mike said, without taking his eyes from the slippery highway. "When it comes to driving in storms, you are talking to *the* driver of the business. You *may* call me superstar—if you wish." He glanced at his partner with a grin, and Rollie groaned.

"As if we don't have enough problems, and now this," Rollie said with mock disgust. "Okay, super, drive on."

"This should be interesting," Mike said as they turned north on the gravel. They were headed directly into the wind and the narrow road was dotted with rapidly growing drifts.

"Looks like someone's tried to go through this way already," he said, more to himself than to Rollie. "I'm going to try to stay in those tracks as long as possible to cut down the chances of getting hung up. They aren't much, but they could make the difference."

Rollie just nodded, tensing as they plowed through a drift.

"All units," the dispatcher paused. "Current information is update on weather and road conditions as of zero-eight-thirty. Weather Bureau reports eight inches of new snow on the ground with winds constant at fifteen to twenty miles-per-hour, gusting to forty miles-per-hour. Predictions are for four to eight inches of new snow during the next eight to ten hours with winds diminishing toward evening and temperatures falling below zero. Weather Bureau advises against travel with roads snow-packed and slippery."

"Oh, great!" Mike muttered. "Surely you jest, wise weather bureau. It's just like summer out here!" He laughed wryly and Rollie joined in.

They passed the first crossroad. A mile down and two to go, Rollie thought. "Damn!" The car started to skid and Mike cursed as he fought the wheel, finally bringing it back in line on the road's center. The tire tracks ahead had vanished. Rollie sighed, saying nothing.

As they reached the second crossroad, the constant battering the car was taking from the wind suddenly increased sharply. "It's the wind. . . ." Mike's voice trailed off as he struggled with the steering wheel. The car went sideways, spun completely around and backwards into the driver's-side ditch, then stalled.

"Fuck!"

Rollie stared at his partner in reproach. It was one word he didn't like to hear, but he kept his feelings to himself.

With a look of disgust, Mike turned the key and the engine roared back to life. He shifted the car in super low and eased his foot onto the gas pedal. The car shuddered but did not move. "Well, we're hung up good. Damnit!" He slammed his open palm against the steering wheel. "Rollie? What the hell are we going to do?"

"We got the shovels?"

Mike nodded.

Rollie zipped up his jacket and opened the door. "Let's give them a try." He battled the wind to the rear of the car and waited for Mike to open the trunk. They pulled the shovels free and slammed down the lid. Rollie motioned to the driver's side and Mike nodded and started to dig under the wheels.

Rollie crunched the shovel blade into the packed snow on his own side. He ducked behind the car as he dug, trying to gain some protection, but the snow kept swirling around the car and into his face. His face began feeling as if it were being jabbed by needles as the wind continued whipping the snow. He blinked away the tears. Finally, gasping for breath, he climbed back into the car, still holding the shovel.

Seconds later, Mike joined him. They sat silently, catching their breath, then Mike slammed the car into gear and once again tried to wrench it free. No response. Without speaking, he pulled the gear shift to reverse, but still the car would not move. Roaring the engine, he finally eased off and shifted back to neutral. "How far you think to the Schmidt farm?" The words came in gasps.

Rollie shrugged. "Three-quarters, maybe only half a mile. Maybe we should try to walk it."

"Maybe. And maybe there's a highway department rig or tow truck in the area, too. Let's call it in." He picked off the mike. "Zebra base, this is Zebra-Nine."

"Go ahead."

"We're hung up on the gravel about a mile from the Schmidt farm. Are there tow vehicles in our zone?"

"Negative." There was a pause. "We can send help in about . . ." another pause, "an hour."

Mike and Rollie exchanged glances. "Cancel that, Zebra base. We'll try to dig out and keep you advised."

"Ten-four."

Rollie exhaled loudly.

"Dig some more, or what?" Mike asked.

"No, I'll walk," Rollie replied. "It's eight-forty-five. If I haven't returned with Schmidt in an hour, get on the horn and get some help out here. And stick with the car!" Mike nodded. "How's the gas?" Rollie asked.

"About half."

"Okay, that'll hold for a while. And don't worry, I'm sure I can make it through." Rollie snapped the fur-covered hat down over his ears and zipped up his coat.

"Rollie, maybe you shouldn't. . . ."

"Don't worry! I'll make it!" Rollie's confidence was up. He'd tried difficult things before—that's how he'd built his reputation. He thought Mike looked skeptical, but he ignored the look. Time to move. He climbed out and began walking.

The wind was killing. He tried to look up as he walked, but the driving snow forced him to keep his head down. He fought for every step, moving around the drifts and using the frozen gravel for footing. He tried walking backwards. By now, the car was out of sight. How far had he come? Had he been walking a few minutes? Or was it longer? He'd check his watch soon. He felt like he was making good progress, but the wind was beginning to take its toll on his legs and face. He pulled the coat collar up as far as possible and faced back into the wind. His lungs began to ache from the cold air.

He stopped. This was ridiculous. He'd never make it to the farm. He looked around. Aside from the small bit of visible road, all he could see was the fence line on the other side of the ditch. He pursed his lips in renewed determination. No time to panic, he could make it. What the hell, it couldn't be that much farther.

He was walking slower now and his legs really hurt. He stopped again, turned, then turned back. Going back—that would be a loser's way out. No, by God, he'd make it! He rubbed his thighs to get the circulation going. How much farther? The doubts returned as he trudged on. His lungs and face were on fire, and his legs were numb. How could this be happening so fast?

"I haven't been out here that long!" he shouted into the wind to reinforce himself, then moved on. God! It hurt! It *really* hurt! He stopped again. The tears welled up, this time from self-pity. He was getting scared. He tried to look up the road.

Nothing. Only snow. A layer of ice was forming on his eyebrows. The snow was no longer melting when it hit his face.

For some strange reason, he felt like crying. He sank to his knees and turned his back to the wind. Stupid! Stupid pride! He cried quietly. His body felt numb. "Can't let myself freeze." He tried to stand, but his legs wouldn't react. He flailed his arms and found them growing numb, too. He kept working them and they began to hurt. Good! He'd read that was good, although he couldn't think of any reason why. It hurt like hell! He laughed, almost hysterically, then cried some more. Now he couldn't feel anything in his legs.

He sat still, not knowing what to do, then he heard a noise. At least it sounded different from the constant howling of the wind. He turned his head back into the wind. It was there again. A growling noise. It grew louder. He wasn't sure what it was, but it sounded like some sort of engine. He kept his head turned into the wind. The biting cold on his cheek forgotten.

At first it was just a shadow between the gusts of wind and snow, then it got clearer. It was a farm tractor. Rollie began yelling maniacally. His arms felt like lead but he still brought one up to shoulder height in a weak wave. The tractor almost roared on by before sliding to a halt. A well-bundled figure climbed down from the glassed-in cab.

"Glad . . . to-to-see . . . you," Rollie said weakly.

"Come on! Can you stand?"

Rollie shook his head.

"Okay, then hang on!" The farmer shouted over the wind, then ran back to his tractor and turned it around. A manure loader was hooked to the front of the tractor, and he lowered it to the ground before returning to Rollie's side. Then he reached down and picked Rollie up. Walking unevenly to the loader, he placed Rollie firmly in the loader's front-end bucket. "Hang on!" He shouted again and left.

Rollie did not move. Suddenly, he found himself rolling back on the frozen manure as the farmer tilted the bucket and joisted it in the air. Rollie was so cold he barely felt the bucket's jolts as they sped along. He wondered who had him and where they were going. As if in answer to his thoughts, the tractor slid to a stop and he felt himself being lowered to the ground.

Once again the man picked him up bodily and walked to the door of a medium-sized frame house. A middle-aged woman held the door wide as the farmer bumped and banged himself and Rollie inside. They continued straight to what looked like the living room and the farmer laid him down on the carpet. Rollie was shivering violently.

"Get his hat. I'll get his coat," the farmer said to his wife. They worked together to strip off Rollie's outer clothing, then began chaffing his arms and legs. Rollie cried out in pain, then lay back as they ignored him.

"How you feelin'?" The muscular man, with a drawn, weather-beaten face and day's growth of whiskers, kept rubbing Rollie's legs as he looked up to ask.

"B-b-better," he answered. "Real-really cold yet. N-n-numb."

"My name's Howard Schmidt," the man said. "Got a call from Doc Jonas that there'd be some help on the way for my son. Got a little worried when you didn't get here when he said, so thought I'd come on out and see if you were hung up on one of them drifts. Looks like maybe you were."

"Y-yes, I . . . m-my partner . . . h-h-he's still w-with the car." Rollie was shaking violently again.

Schmidt stopped rubbing. "Where?" He stood up.

"B-back up . . . the road. Mmm-m-maybe three qua-quarters of a m-mile. I-I left him . . . s-started walking . . . eight-forty-five. I-I-I h-had to stop. F-freezing."

"Eight-forty-five." Schmidt looked at his watch. "Well, it's twenty to ten now. I'll hop on the tractor and head back up and get him. You keep working on this one," he said to his wife, then looked at Rollie. "What's your name?"

"Patterson. I-I thought I could make it, b-b-but got t-t-too cold. Can you r-reach m-my partner okay?"

"I can get through with the tractor. You know," he stopped as he turned to go and added, "you were only about a hundred yards from the driveway." He shook his head. "A hundred yards, and you coulda froze." He walked to the door and left.

"Howard'll get your partner and be back in no time," his wife said as Rollie watched him go. "We've been waiting for you to get here. Our boy's in bad shape. Got the measles. We'll need you to take him in for us. Howard can get you and your car in and out with that big tractor. Is the highway open?"

"Enough," Rollie answered, shuddering but feeling much better as she continued massaging his arms and neck. "Your l-l-little b-boy? How bad is he?"

"He's got a real bad fever. Real bad." She shook her head. "He's been vomiting some now, too. We need to get him in, but the tractor's the only thing that can move in and out. We tried the pickup, but it's old an' froze up. Couldn't get it to run no how."

She rose and walked into an adjoining room, returning with a blanket. Draping it around Rollie's shoulders, she helped him get up and then over to a chair. His legs ached with the movement. She brought him a steaming cup of coffee, which he gulped gratefully, feeling the hot liquid burning all the way to his stomach. He gulped at it some more, ignoring the scalding he was administering to the inside of his mouth.

It was just about ten when the tractor pulled into the farm yard towing the patrol car. Schmidt and Henson came quickly inside.

Schmidt's wife hurried from the bedroom where she had been sponging her son. "Howard, he's real bad!" She nodded quickly to Mike to acknowledge his presence, then turned back to the bedroom. Schmidt followed, leaving Mike stranded in the kitchen. Henson peered into the living room, then continued in when he saw Rollie.

"Schmidt told me," he said quickly, cutting Rollie off before he could speak. "How you feeling?"

Rollie nodded weakly, trying to avoid Mike's "I told you so" stare.

"You know you look like shit!"

Rollie started and looked up. He had expected consolation—not this.

"You're a good cop. A damn good cop!" Mike said, pacing in front of him. "But I don't need any dead-hero partners. Especially on a day like this! *God*, look at you! Damn, Rollie. . . ." He swung around, then back, then put a hand on Rollie's shoulder. "Damn . . . " he said hoarsely. He backed away and began pacing again.

Rollie looked and felt miserable huddling under the blanket. He watched Mike silently, not knowing how to react. "Mike, I . . . I'm . . . "

Mike turned quickly. "Forget it, man, forget it." He put a hand back on Rollie's shoulder.

"But I. . . ." Rollie started to explain how he felt.

Mike waved a hand before his face. "You gonna complete this patrol?"

Rollie shivered, then nodded.

"Me too." He dismissed the apology still on Rollie's lips by turning and walking back into the kitchen where he helped himself to a cup and poured some coffee.

"Can we take my son?" Rollie looked over his shoulder to see Schmidt standing in the bedroom doorway, holding his son in his arms.

Mike hurried into the room at the sound of Schmidt's voice.

"Yeah, get him to the car. You get us to the highway; we'll make the hospital." He nodded a reassurance he didn't feel.

Schmidt looked scared. His son lay limply in his arms, blankets surrounding him. The boy's face was scarlet and his breathing strangled. His eyes were closed tightly.

"Is his temperature high?" Rollie spoke while standing, tossing aside the blanket. He walked shakily to the door, then came back to pick up his discarded hat and coat.

"I don't know. He's really hot. We don't have no thermometer. The Missus has been sponging him to try to cool him off. We better go!"

Rollie and Mike nodded in unison and Mike looked to Rollie questioningly. Rollie pulled on the coat in reply and Mike nodded again and left for the car. Rollie walked to the door, hurting with every step, and held it ajar for the farmer.

His son opened his eyes and stared at the pale patrolman. "Dad, you takin' me to the hospital?"

"Yes, son," Schmidt answered as he walked to the door.

"Okay," the boy responded and closed his eyes again. "Dad?"

Schmidt stopped.

"We better take that man over there too. He don't look so good."

"You know, I'd like to try to call Jean and see how she's doing." Rollie walked stiffly to a chair near the hospital elevator door and sat down.

"Go ahead and try from the desk," Mike replied. "I'll get this." He waved the emergency report the nurse had handed them when they brought the Schmidt boy in. "Then we'll hit it again."

"Thanks." Rollie dragged himself to his feet. He felt better, though a lot like he often did the day after a strenuous workout. His muscles ached. "Oh . . . here." He turned back and unhooked the portable radio. "In case."

Mike took the radio and laid it on the chair beside him, then waved Rollie on without looking up from the report.

The nurse looked up expectantly.

"I'd like to try to call my home phone number. Would it be all right to place a quick call from that phone?" He pointed to the one on the reception desk.

"Oh, certainly," she smiled, shoving it toward him.

Rollie dialed quickly, smiling at her as he waited for the number to connect. Busy. He depressed the button and dialed again. Still busy.

"No luck?" The nurse looked up.

"Uh, no. Seems to be busy. Mind if I wait and try again?"

"Of course, just as long as you space out the calls."

Rollie drummed his fingers nervously on the counter top, then dialed a third time. Still busy. He looked at his watch. Already after eleven. He dialed again, then let the receiver slide onto the cradle as the busy signal rasped out at him.

Mike walked up and touched his arm. "We've got a call."

He reached over and handed the nurse the completed report. "A guy from the Phillips Company called in. Says his truck driver checked in about 4 A.M. and was on his way here from Center Point by way of Highway 34. So far, the driver hasn't showed."

"Was the driver at Center Point then?"

"Yeah, and it can't be more than three hours on a good day. Double it today and he's running a little over."

"Might just be playing it safe."

"Yeah, maybe, but his boss thinks he's in trouble out there. What do you think?"

Rollie looked back at the phone, then picked it up and dialed again. He hung up slowly. "Maybe it's a problem and maybe not," he mused, still eyeing the phone. "Wonder who she's talking to for so long?"

"What?" Mike asked.

"Oh . . . nothing. Line's been busy ever since I started trying."

"Well, maybe we should wait. . . ." Mike waited for Rollie's decision. "Maybe there's really no problem with that truck driver, you know."

"No, no. I'll try later. I'm sure everything's fine." He took the keys from Mike's hand. "Come on. It's my turn to drive."

CHAPTER FIVE

Lorre and Jack had been walking more than two hours when the accident occurred. It was a freak sort of thing, a once-in-a-lifetime accident which brings out the laughs later when it's retold how it happened. Only on this night it happened to two men on the run, dissipating any humor as far as they were concerned.

It probably wouldn't have happened at all if a car hadn't chosen this particular night to take the dirt road they were wearily walking along. One moment they were walking with heads bowed into the wind, the next they were scrambling into the underbrush as the lights swung up and over a hill ahead of them and bore down. They ran side by side, pushing through the branches and brambles, then crouched together about 100 feet off the road.

Lorre listened to Jack's heavy breathing as he

watched the car approach, then he heard the click of the revolver's hammer. "What are you doing?" He whirled to face his partner, grasping his own gun in the process and grabbing Jack's arm.

"Just making sure—in case it's a cop or something. Gotta be sure." Jack took a deep breath, quieting his previous sharp breathing.

"A cop or something! Hell! It's probably some farmer or teenager. Put that damn thing away and stay quiet! He couldn't see us here even if he was a cop."

Jack shook his arm free and peered between the bushes at the now clearly visible headlights inching down the road. The driver was moving slowly to avoid sliding on the road's surface, slimy from the rain. Jack eased up on the hammer but kept the weapon in his hand. Lorre grunted and slipped his gun back into his belt. They waited.

The car was a newer model, the familiar badges of authority—the red light, spot light, and emblem were missing. It whined softly as it moved down the center of the road, passing in line with the two men but not slowing. Each man breathed a sigh of relief as it passed.

Jack stood and put the gun away. "You see any markings on that car?"

"No, but it could have been the police anyway, you never know. If they're looking, they might see the ambulance."

"Yeah, I know. As slow as they're driving, they might see it even if they're not looking." Jack looked again at the now-dimming tail lights as he spoke.

"We'd better stick to the fields for a while and hope we find a farm house that way. Christ! There's got to be someplace around here! I've never seen anything *this* desolate!"

Lorre thought quickly back to his own small town and the rolling miles of empty countryside surrounding it. "Back home, we'd call this God's country. Never really considered it desolate."

"You call it what the fuck you like," Schumacher snapped. "But it looks a lot more like hell than any sort of God's country! I guess about the only thing that keeps it from being called hell is this damn cold!" He shivered and rubbed his arms across his chest. "Are we gonna stand around bitching while we freeze to death, or we going?"

"Who's bitching?" Lorre asked. He stopped shivering and took a deep breath of the rain-washed air. "Yeah, we're going."

"Which way?" Jack asked, scowling at the tangle of brush and trees.

"Why not continue straight out?" Lorre said. "The brush can't last too long 'cause the trees are only along the road. We should be able to see something once we get out on the prairie—maybe even spot a farm house or some buildings."

They began walking, shoving aside the branches and dead vines as they moved. The rain picked up in intensity, occasionally joined by a heavy, wet snowflake. Jack cursed from time to time as his feet caught in the vines or a blast of icy wind buffeted them. The snow had started falling with regularity by the time they reached the edge of the trees and started up a grassy knoll. Overhead it was still black, but in the east, the sky was graying.

They stopped for a breather, not talking. Then, as if on signal, they rose and continued uphill. The wind was swirling the snow around them, making visibility tougher. Even the lighter gray of the east was disappearing. They were soon enveloped in a swirling gray-white.

Lorre stopped and stared at his watch—nearly 4 A.M.

"We've got to find some shelter soon, or we won't get out of this!" Jack shouted back to him.

"Well, we're bound to come on a farm soon—hang on!"

"No! Hell with a farm! We've got to look for something else—any kind of shelter before this snow gets worse or the temperature drops. Anything's better than tramping around like this!" Jack gestured with his arms wide apart as he shouted.

"Well ... what?" Lorre asked, dropping to his knees to avoid some of the wind.

"How the fuck should I know! Jesus Christ, you're the big country boy. You tell me what will keep us out of the wind!" He whirled and looked around, started to sit down, then looked back up the hill. "Hey ... what was that?"

"What?" Lorre looked at him disgustedly.

"That! I saw something moving up there." He pulled the gun from his belt as he spoke, pointing toward the crest of the hill. Lorre looked past him and saw a slight blur of movement. Jack crouched and began creeping forward. Lorre, too, crouched but did not move, watching Jack crabwalking toward the hilltop.

Suddenly, Jack leaped up and fired, then ran quickly on, disappearing from view. Lorre heard a second shot, then silence. He advanced cautiously, stopping at the spot where Jack had first fired. He could see nothing. He eased ahead, keeping his gun ready, but uncocked. He had gone about 100 feet when he saw something move. A few more steps revealed a body; a few more and he could see it was Jack.

"What happened?" He rushed forward and crouched at Jack's side, keeping the gun loose.

"My leg—my foot!" Jack moaned loudly.

Lorre looked down at Jack's foot and saw the blood seeping from a hole in the shoe. "I slipped when I ran forward and the gun went off. God! My foot must be broken!" He grabbed his right leg with both hands and moaned again.

"What the hell were you shooting at?" Lorre was still looking around as he spoke.

"I don't know. Could've been a man. Still up ahead."

Lorre eased past his partner and moved on, staying low and alert. Suddenly his heart jumped as a flurry of movement erupted in front of him. Then he laughed loudly, stood up and walked back to Schumacher's side. "It was a goddamn rabbit!" He laughed louder. "Can you believe that? You shot yourself chasing a stinking rabbit!"

He tried to stifle his laughter as he looked at Jack

writhing in pain but failed and guffawed loudly. "That's damn near the funniest thing I've heard of in three years." He gasped for breath as he laughed.

"You sonofabitch!" Jack yelled, still holding his leg. "I'm laying here bleeding to death and you stand there laughing. I oughta put a bullet in you just to see how the hell you like it!" As he spoke, he jerked the gun up from beside him on the ground.

Instantly, Lorre lashed out with his foot, knocking the gun away. He glared down at his wounded partner, forgetting his amusement from a few seconds before. "Don't ever do that again," he said coldly. "If you do, I'll break your arm like I'd break a toothpick." He stared evenly into Schumacher's eyes until Jack nodded, displaying a look of fear for the first time since the escape had started. "Now, let me look at that foot."

Lorre pulled Jack's shoe free and eyed the wound. Without speaking, he ripped a corner off Jack's blanket, then wrapped it tightly around the foot. Pulling the shoelace loose, he strung it over and around the piece of blanket and knotted it firmly near the ankle. Jack yelled in pain, but Lorre kept working. He picked up the laceless shoe and forced it back onto the foot, ignoring still another scream. Then, brushing the snow from Jack's legs, he slipped his arms under Jack's and lifted him to his feet. "Try putting some weight on that foot!"

Jack stepped down, groaned and shook his head. "Too much pain. I can't."

"Then get your arm over my shoulder," Lorre ordered, supporting him. "We've got to keep moving before your foot and the blizzard get any worse."

They stepped off slowly, still moving in the same direction again. Their progress was painfully slow. They paused every few minutes as Lorre readjusted Jack's weight and tried to note the lay of the land and locate any form of shelter. There was none. An hour passed, then two. The pair looked like walking snowmen and their mustaches became caked with ice from their heavy breathing. Neither spoke, although several times Jack's moaning overcame the wind's howl. Lorre knew they couldn't go much farther without some sort of shelter. His hands felt frozen. He had lost his feeling in them. His legs, too, were growing stiff.

Then, like a miracle, the shelter was there. One second, there was the constant gray and white, the next, an outline of a grove of trees. Lorre nearly dragged Jack the final few yards, dropping gratefully out of the wind into the grove's shelter. He looked around, then cried out in joy. Only yards away, past the trees, was a building.

"Jack . . . Jack . . . come on. Look!" He lifted Jack and pointed to the building. Jack struggled to rise, the haggard look on his face turning to one of desperation—a need to reach that building.

They crawled to the building's side. Jack sat gasping with his back to the wall, while Lorre moved to the corner and looked around. More buildings. Two for sure, and a house across an open yard. He looked along the side of the shed. Two doors. He hurried along the side and found the larger one chained shut. The second opened easily. He looked at the house. It was dark.

"There's more buildings," he said, returning to Jack's side. "One's a house."

"Let's go there," Jack said quickly, trying to stand.

"No!" Lorre gasped. "No, not yet. Don't know who's in there. Let's get inside here first, then think it over. Come on." He pulled Jack to his feet. Working cautiously, they finally reached the small door and got inside. The house was still dark. He looked at his watch: six-forty-five.

Jack fell against the wall and sank to the ground. His hands were white with streaks of blue. He had not tried to warm them at the grove.

Lorre's hands were numb but he could flex them now, better than before. He looked outside. There was no movement from the house. He shut the door and sat down.

They sat that way for forty-five minutes. Jack never stopped shaking, but Lorre's shivering subsided. Lorre got up and pain shot through his legs. The cold was wearing off. It was fairly warm in the shed. He walked stiffly around. Besides the old truck, there were several old cattle feedbunks, some hog troughs, and miscellaneous farm tools. More tools and boards were stored in a small loft.

He checked the truck. No key, but that could be remedied. The door chained shut would be a problem, though. He thought again of the house.

"Wonder if they've got a dog?" he asked aloud as he walked back to the door. He opened it a crack and stared at the house. There were lights on now, and the sky was light, too. It was snowing harder. "Someone's up in the house now. Can't see who's moving around, though."

Jack looked up slowly but did not respond. Lorre walked over and checked his foot. It was hard to tell how badly it was swollen with the blanket tied inside the shoe. He rubbed at Jack's frozen hands, then pushed them under the blanket poncho.

Lorre paced some more, stepping to the door every few minutes to look out. He checked his watch again. Eight-twenty. The house door opened and a woman stepped out onto the porch.

"Jack. Someone's coming!" Lorre ran to his partner's side. Jack rolled his eyes in response and groaned. "Come on! We've got to hide!" Lorre dragged him to his feet, slapping a hand over Jack's mouth to stifle any groans or possible screams. He looked around the shed wildly, then stumbled toward the feedbunks. Picking Jack up, he shoved him into a bunk. "Lay still!" he ordered. Schumacher nodded weakly.

Lorre looked toward the door then dived into the other bunk, lying flat on his back. He could hear the door opening. The creak of the pickup door caused him to start but he remained still. The truck engine roared.

Should he make his move? Before he could decide, the engine went dead and the creaking noise came again. The door reopened and closed. He sat up, then climbed quickly from the bunk and ran to the door and looked out. The woman was halfway back to the house.

"Jack! Come on! It's a woman and I think she's by herself. She's got a key for this truck." Lorre talked excitedly, hurrying to help Jack from the bunk.

"Look, I . . . I don't think I can. . . ." Jack stared weakly at him.

"You'll make it. I'll get you there," Lorre snapped. "I'll get you to the front, then I'll get around to the back. I don't care if you have to crawl, but you'll make it or, by God, I'll leave you here to freeze to death!"

Jack shuddered, then leaned on Lorre for support, signifying he'd go. It took nearly ten minutes to move the 100 yards from the shed to the house. Several times Lorre thought of dumping Jack to the ground and rushing on before they were seen.

When they reached the edge of the porch, he still wondered if they'd been spotted. "You get to the front door and don't let anyone out. You got that?"

Jack nodded.

"Okay." Lorre said it more to himself, then sprinted around the corner toward the back.

A minute passed, then Jack grabbed the edge of the porch and pulled himself up. The pain was almost unbearable as he put his weight on the injured foot. He sobbed softly to himself, then gritted his teeth and went on. Dropping to his knees, he crawled the the final few yards. Using the handle of the door as a brace, he pulled himself to his feet, then leaned against the door and waited. He laughed softly to himself, for no reason, then sobbed again. He bowed his head slightly.

The force of the door being jerked open nearly

knocked him down, and he found himself face-to-face with a young woman. She screamed. He reached to grab a swinging fist, but it was gone as she fell in a heap at his feet. He stared stupidly at her, then looked up to see Lorre approaching. The room began swirling. He moved an arm in front of him toward the door, trying to grab the knob, then blacked out.

CHAPTER SIX

The gnawing pain in Jean's stomach was the first thing she was conscious of as she regained her senses. She reached down to feel her stomach, but the pain receded. Then she remembered the men and sat up sharply.

She was lying on the living room couch. The men were both staring at her. One looked little-boyish, despite his size, because of the set of Rollie's clothes he had found and was wearing. The other appeared to be in pain. He was wrapped in a blanket and sitting before a heat vent, shivering. Neither spoke. The big one picked up a coffee cup from the end table, took a sip and carefully replaced it. He looked around nervously.

"Who are you?" The words wavered as she spoke them, and Jean tried to conceal her fear as she continued. "And what are you doing here? Why are you wearing my husband's clothes?"

The man in the blanket glowered but did not speak. It was the big one who finally replied. "It's no concern of yours who we are. All we want is some food, a chance to get dry, and the keys to that shed out there—and that truck. Other than that, you don't need to worry." He stood. "Oh, and we'll need to take care of my friend's foot here. He's had an accident."

"I think you'd both better leave—now!" Jean demanded, standing and feeling braver. She looked at her watch, emphasizing the movement. It was nearly ten—several hours before Rollie would be home. "My husband will be home any minute now—and he's with the police!"

The man in the blanket whipped around at the word, while the tall one walked to the window and looked out. The snow was heavier than ever. He turned back toward her. "So your husband's a cop. That's really too bad, because if he's fool enough to drive home in this storm, well, then, we'll just have to use you as our shield against him." He glanced at the other man, who pulled his gun free from the blanket.

Jean stifled a small scream, holding both hands over her mouth. Then she shifted them to her stomach and doubled over, sitting back down on the couch. She gasped as the pain ran through her body, then breathed easier as it passed.

The big man came to her side. "Are you all right?" His appearance of concern helped Jean relax somewhat. She nodded.

"Put that damn thing away. Don't you think we could hear him if he drove up?" He turned and spat the words at the man in the blanket, scowling as he spoke. "Now, when does your husband usually come home?" he asked, turning and looking straight at Jean while he waited for her reply. "Usually about now, but if it's snowing hard, he'll probably be late and call to make sure I'm okay or something."

"Then he'll find the line busy." He walked to the phone and held up the line which had been ripped free from the phone jack. "Where does he work?"

Jean paused, trying to think of some way to stall them, but it seemed useless. "Hollysberg," she mumbled.

"Hollysberg. How far from here is that?"

"Twenty miles or so."

"Twenty . . . hell, there's no way he's going to get home on time going that far in this. . . ." He waved an arm toward the window.

"Yeah, but what if he does?" It was the first time the man in the blanket had spoken, and Jean watched him closely as the hoarse words came out. "Let's get the hell out of here and on the road—soon!"

"Yeah, all right," the big one answered, rubbing at his chin, "but first we gotta fix that foot. You know any doctoring?" He directed the question to Jean, who nodded.

"A little—mostly first aid, but. . . ." She doubled over again unable to complete the sentence. This time the pain lasted nearly thirty seconds before subsiding.

"Lady, what's wrong?" The big man knelt at her side.

"I think I'm going into labor," Jean gasped as the pain eased. "These pains are coming pretty regularly. The baby's not due for a month yet, but that has to be it. I don't know. . . ." She let the sentence trail off as she looked up at him. His face had softened and he looked worried.

"Who are you, anyway?" she asked.

"My name's Lorre. That's Jack. That's all you need to know. Look, we'll get fixed up and out of here, then you won't have to worry about us, okay?"

Jean nodded, got up and made her way to Jack's side. He had an angry look on his face, yet she could see he was in obvious pain. "Where are you hurt?"

Jack pointed to his foot. Jean pulled on the shoe and slipped it off, revealing a blood-soaked piece of blanket. She pulled the shoestring loose and began unwinding it.

"Jesus Christ, lady, be careful!"

Jean flinched as the words exploded from Jack. Then she carefully unwound more, stopping as she reached the point where the dried blood caused the blanket to stick to the wound. She could see the powder burns and bits of raw flesh around the wound's edges. "You better hang on to your friend," she said to Lorre. "This will hurt."

"Just get it the hell off, lady, I'll hang on to my own goddamn body!" Jack grabbed the edge of a chair sitting next to him. "Now do it!"

Jean grabbed the blanket and pulled, grimacing at Jack's scream of pain. She tossed the bloodied strip aside and stared at the wound. It was raw, ragged and blackened on the edges from the dried blood. His skin felt very cold. For a second she wanted to vomit, then she shook it off and got up. "We've got to get that cleaned and bandaged properly before it gets infected. How long ago did it happen?"

"This morning sometime. Maybe five-six hours ago," Lorre said. "You want me to do something?"

"Yes. Get the bandages, tape, and gauze from the bathroom—and some towels. I'll get some hot water from the kitchen."

Lorre paused and looked at her.

"Don't worry, I'm not going to try to run away. I'm not stupid, you know. I'm going into labor and I'm not about to freeze to death getting away from you."

Lorre turned and walked on toward the bathroom.

Jean went to the kitchen and filled a pan with lukewarm water, taking a clean dishcloth from one of the drawers. By the time she returned to Jack's side, some blood had oozed onto the floor. Once again her stomach felt queasy, but she fought it off. She barely had the pan onto the floor when another contraction came. Gasping, she grabbed Jack's knee and hung on till the worst had passed. He stared at her with disgust. Lorre returned with the bandages and stood helplessly by, waiting until the pain passed.

Working quickly, she bathed and cleaned the wound as thoroughly as possible. She sent Lorre back to the bathroom for some medicated salve. "This will hurt," she warned Jack as she took the salve. He clenched his teeth and made a hissing sound as she applied it, but this time he did not scream. Jean wrapped the wound with gauze, then overstripped it with tape. She sat back and looked at it proudly. "Not too bad, huh? For an amateur, I mean." She glanced up at Lorre, who returned a faint smile. Jack eyed the bandage and scowled.

"Okay," Lorre said firmly. "Get us something to eat and we'll get out of here. All we need is some soup, or sandwiches, or something like that . . . and some food to take along."

Jean struggled to her feet but hadn't reached the kitchen door when another pain hit her. She nearly fell before Lorre reached her side and helped her back to the couch. "Look, lady," Lorre said nervously, "just tell me where it's at and I'll take care of it."

"The soup's in the cupboard—over the stove," Jean gasped as the pain eased, "and the bread's in the big box on the counter. There's meat and things in the refrigerator."

Lorre left her and went in to prepare the food. The pains came and went twice before he returned, carrying some sandwiches and a loaf of bread with the meat and some cheese wrapped inside. He laid them down and went back for the soup, taking a bowl to Jack, then sitting to eat his own. He watched Jean carefully, nearly rising to help her when another pain came, then deciding against it.

Jack ignored her, eating the soup rapidly and reaching for a sandwich. He belched loudly, then stuffed the remains of the sandwich in his mouth. "I'll need a sock," he said as he chewed. "Soon's I get that and the shoe back on, we can get on the road."

Lorre gave him a look of disdain, then walked to the bedroom. He returned with a pair of socks and tossed them at Jack. Stepping to the closet, he pulled out two of Rollie's heavier coats. Both were too small for him, but he slipped one on, anyway, and tossed the other at Jack's feet.

Jack had nearly finished putting on his shoe when Jean felt the worst of the contractions. She doubled completely over, moaning, then slipped to the floor. "Help me . . . please!" She gasped it out through the pain.

Lorre dropped to one knee at her side and helped her back onto the couch. "Is it getting close, lady?"

She nodded.

"You'll be all right. Don't worry. Your husband should've tried phoning by now and he'll be on his way. I'll bet he'll be here any time. That's why we've gotta go, you know, before he arrives."

Jean sat still, not speaking.

"Where are the keys for the shed and the truck?"

"On top of the shelf . . . over the sink."

Lorre hurried to the kitchen and came back with the keys. "We'll leave you now. Don't worry. Your husband'll. . . ."

Jean screamed, stopping his sentence.

"Holy Jesus, lady! What's wrong? What can we do?" Lorre rushed back to her side.

"It's . . . it's . . . the baby! The baby's close! My God. . . ." She shuddered. "It hurts bad. Real bad!"

She looked into Lorre's eyes. "Please help me," she begged. "Take me to the doctor. You can leave me there and go on." She grabbed his hand. "Please!"

"But your husband. . . ."

"My husband won't be here for several hours. I-I lied about him coming home so soon. His shift isn't even over till two." She moaned again. The contractions were closer together. She was suddenly very afraid.

Lorre looked at Jack. "Leave her. We've got enough problems of our own," Jack snapped. He pulled himself to his feet and tested the bound foot by slowly pushing down on it. "We better try to get to a main road before the snow gets worse." He hobbled painfully toward the door. "Now c'mon, bring those keys and let's get the hell out of here."

Jean clamped her hand down on Lorre's as she endured another contraction. She watched as he patted the hand, then gently pulled his away. "Wait. . . ." He waved at Jack. "Lady, where is the nearest doctor?"

"In Hollysberg."

"Where the goddamn cop station is located! Goddamnit, Lorre, are you nuts? Let's get the fuck out of here, now!" Jack shouted from the door.

"Isn't there anything going the other way?" he asked Jean quietly.

"Maybe," she gasped, "maybe in Marion. About twenty-five miles west."

"Okay," Lorre replied. "We'll take you there. It won't be that big a deal."

Jack turned slowly, accenting the move as he

stepped down on his injured foot. He glared at Lorre for several seconds before speaking. "She's not going with us. Now, do you leave her?" He paused. "Or stay?"

"Neither," Lorre replied. "I already said we'll take her along." He reached over and helped Jean to her feet. "Now, you just lean on me, lady, and everything'll be okay."

It was the click that caused him to pause and sent a shiver down Jean's back. Lorre motioned Jean to sit back down. Once she was settled, he faced his partner and the gun, now aimed at his midsection. Jean gulped. Suddenly she felt very nauseated.

"Don't be crazy, Jack."

"I'm not. I'm not going to risk getting caught and sent back up over some dumb broad whose kid is coming early. I'd just as soon kill both of you as take that chance. Now, just toss me those keys and stay the hell out of my way and everything'll be cool." He waved the gun to emphasize the handing over of the keys.

Lorre pulled them from his pocket, then started at Jean's sob. She watched him move, tense up, then seem to relax as he walked toward his partner. A gesture from the gun stopped him.

"Just hold them out at arm's length and step back!" Jack grabbed the keys and waved Lorre away with the gun.

Lorre backed off three or four steps, brushing his arm against his own gun half covered in his belt. Jean saw him tense again, as if to grab for it, but once again he appeared to relax. He sat down beside her and put an arm around her shoulders as she grimaced again with the pain. Jack edged toward the door and opened it.

"Schumacher."

Jack turned to face them.

"How do you think you're gonna drive the truck with your right foot that way? Ever think of that?"

"Don't worry, I'll manage. You just remember to stay put and you both won't get hurt." He stopped. "Oh, yeah, I almost forgot. I'll take your gun."

Lorre pulled the gun free, started to rise, then tossed it across the room instead. It slid to Jack's feet and stopped. "You want it, you pick it up." Lorre sat back down on the edge of the couch.

Schumacher clenched his teeth in obvious pain as he worked to stoop down and retrieve it. Finally, he kneeled and grabbed it, slipping it into his belt. As he fought to regain his balance and pull himself upright, Lorre leaped toward him. The sudden movement, coupled with Jack's off-balance position, worked to his advantage.

Schumacher whirled and tried to aim, squeezing off the first shot with Lorre only a few feet away. The roar of the gun and Jean's scream filled the room, but the bullet went wildly past Lorre's face and into the wall. Lorre hurtled on, shoulder first, into Schumacher's belly, knocking him back into the door.

The gun went off again, this time sending a bullet straight up into the ceiling. Lorre slapped the gun away, then followed with a roundhouse punch. Jack's jaw gave with the blow and blood spurted from the corner of his mouth. Lorre quickly swung again, slamming home a second punch to Jack's now-exposed mid-section. The fist went deep into the soft flesh and Jack's shocked "ohhh" was the last sound he made. He dropped unconscious to the floor.

Lorre stood and pulled Jack away from the door. He picked up his gun, retrieved the keys, then returned to the couch to help Jean.

"My coat . . . it's there . . . in the closet," she gasped.

He pulled the coat out, helped her into it, then led her to the door. The abrupt step into the bright whiteness of the snowstorm stopped them momentarily as they adjusted their eyes, then they walked on toward the shed.

Halfway there, Jean grabbed at his arm from the pain. They struggled on to the door. He found the padlock key and shoved aside the large sliding door. Picking her up again, he carried her to the truck's passenger side and placed her inside. Then he moved to the driver's side and climbed in.

"You've gotta pump it," Jean puffed, "twice."

Lorre nodded, pumped the footfeed and cranked over the engine. It whined, caught, sputtered, then held. He grunted his satisfaction and shifted into reverse, glancing over his shoulder as he backed out. Once clear of the shed, Lorre pulled the truck around toward the house. "Which way now?" He glanced at Jean.

"Just . . . just past the house . . . then turn left. You'll see the gate there. The main highway's about a mile," she directed.

"Okay," He eased the truck ahead, nursing it forward so it wouldn't start spinning in the snow. Through the snow they could see maybe sixty yards ahead. As they approached the house, there was a movement at the door and Jack hobbled out. There was no sound, but the flash of the exploding gun was clearly visible as Jack fired, shattering the windshield.

Lorre hit the brake, sliding the truck to a stop. "Get down!"

Jean bent toward him at the command as another bullet hit the windshield. Lorre swung open the door, keeping most of his body behind it as he stepped onto the running board. Jack was coming at the truck, gun before him, hobbling painfully and nearly falling.

Lorre shouted over the top of the door, causing Jack to slow down. "Don't be a damn fool! Get the hell out of our way, or get in and ride. This lady's in trouble and I'm taking her to a doctor!"

Jean sat up again and stared toward Jack. "Damnit, get your head down!" Lorre half pushed her below window level then leaned back out to face Jack. The wind was driving the snow straight into Lorre's face. He blinked but kept his position.

Jack looked up, his expression more chilling than the snow-filled wind. They stared at one another for a split second, then Jack fired.

Lorre felt his arm being pulled away from the door before he felt the searing pain run through his left shoulder. He stared briefly at the arm, then quickly back to Jack. The door window shattered at that instant as another bullet struck. Lorre dived into the cab and grunted with pain as he reached out to drag the door shut.

Stomping down on the clutch, he shifted into gear, muttered again to Jean to stay down, then floored the footfeed. The truck careened wildly as the tires dug down toward solid ground. Lorre fought for control, keeping one eye on the almost invisible driveway, and watching for Jack with the other. He saw another flash to his left and involuntarily ducked. The bullet crunched into the truck's body. The fishtailing rear end came back around hard to the left. Lorre fought the wheel, then felt and heard a soft thud.

Glancing quickly over his shoulder, he saw Jack reel off the truck's side and fall into the snow. Jack raised himself partially on an elbow and fired another shot. Ducking again, Lorre heard the bullet smack into the cab wall behind him. He did not look back again, but concentrated instead on the wheel, finally gaining control as he sped through the gate and guided the truck into the road's center.

He looked over to Jean. She was still bent toward him, watching him closely, a look of terror in her eyes. He nodded and motioned for her to sit up and she did, holding her abdomen. Lorre reached across to place a reassuring hand on her shoulder and was painfully reminded of his hurt shoulder as he tried to steer with his left hand. Regrasping the wheel with his right hand, he looked at his arm. Blood was running down the outside of the coat.

CHAPTER SEVEN

"Now, listen, damnit. We're going to need the nearest plow soon or we're going to need the nearest ambulance. I don't give a damn *whose* car is caught in *what* ditch! If you don't get a plow to our position, we're going to have one *very* frozen trucker on our hands!" Mike snapped off the transmitter in disgust then remashed the button down hard and shouted, "Over!"

He looked at Rollie with exasperation. They'd been sitting before a three-foot drift for more than twenty minutes and continuously radioing for a snow-plow to get them through.

"Zebra Nine...." It was Sergeant Granzetti's voice replacing the dispatcher's monotone.

"Go ahead," Mike answered.

There was a pause on the dispatcher's end as Granzetti digested the unorthodox response, then his gravelly voice came back across. "All right, Zebra Nine, we've got a plow on its way to your location. He should arrive within the next twenty minutes. Are you sure that's the road your driver is supposed to be on?"

"That's affirmative!" Mike said emphatically. They had explained their situation five times to the dispatcher.

"All right, Zebra Nine. Relax. It's tight all over today and we're doing the best we can. Understood?"

"Ten-four!" Mike replied, clamping the mike savagely back on its hook. "Goddamnit! Where's that highway support we're supposed to be getting? We might as well be digging our way through with shovels!" He picked up his gloves from the seat, wrung them between his hands, then tossed them back.

It had taken Rollie nearly forty-five minutes to nurse the patrol car twenty-three miles along the iced-over highway. The drifts had been small to this point, but the one blocking them seemed to be growing by the minute.

"If that plow comes shovel down, we'll at least have a clear road back," Rollie said, trying to cheer his partner. "It can't be the plows' fault we're getting hung up like this," he added. "You know as well as I do that the bureaucracy is tying them up pulling the bigwigs out."

"Yeah, yeah. . . ." Mike answered, cooling down. "But, damnit, Rollie, we could have a dead man on our hands up here because of this delay. Shit, man, I wish I was in some sort of position of power! I'd let them freeze their asses and their cars in their big fancy driveways." He peeled back his sleeve and looked at his watch and Rollie followed suit. It was ten minutes to noon.

"You know, this might be a helluva time to say it, but I'm hungry," Rollie said as Mike continued looking at his watch.

"We'll grab something next time in. It shouldn't take long to find this guy once we get a plow in front of us. We'll hang onto him and get him to lead the way back, too. With a clear road, things'll speed up. Hey, with all this waiting around, I gotta go!" He jerked up the zipper of his jacket and stepped out. Rollie leaned back, waiting, while his partner relieved himself in the snow alongside the road.

"Whew! I'm glad we've got that radio or we might be in a helluva mess out here," Mike gasped as he climbed back in. "Must really be poor out there in the open." He jerked a thumb toward the side, indicating the open fields beyond the ditch. "Those side roads have gotta be gone by now."

"You think so?" Rollie said sharply, sitting straighter behind the wheel. "I'm still planning to get home tonight, you know."

"I wouldn't count on it if I were you, man. Those winds are gonna pile that snow a lot deeper over the next couple of hours. And if Granzetti decides to keep us on for part of that next shift . . . hell, you might as well write it off."

Rollie leaned back again. "Sure hope Jean'll be okay. It bothers me—her being alone in weather like this and the baby so close. What if something happens?" He looked worriedly at Mike.

"Hey, don't get so uptight over the little things. Hell, man, didn't you just tell me she's a whole month away? Anyway, she's got the phone and that 'super' heating system you've been bragging up, so what's to worry? If she's got problems, she'll call the hospital and they'll contact the station and let you know, right?"

"Yeah, I guess so," Rollie answered. "Still. . . ."

"Aw, *still* nothing. Come on, sitting around here's got your brain gummed up. Don't worry. Even if you end up in town overnight, you'll be able to check with her by phone."

"Sure, that's what I was sayin'. I wish I could have reached her back there at the hospital. Maybe I should've taken a few more minutes and tried to get through before we headed out. If I'd have known we were going to sit around in front of a damn snow drift this long, I would've taken the time." He looked glumly at his partner. "You think everything's all right though, huh?"

"Positive. Now quit worrying."

Rollie grinned. "Yeah, you're probably right. Guess I'm just a little edgy with this storm hanging on like it is. I'm going to call her right away, though, when we get in."

"Okay," Mike replied, leaning back against the door to relax. "Hey! Lights!"

"Where?" Rollie looked back over his shoulder through the rear window, then saw the flash between gusts. The blinking lights grew larger as the plow bore down on them, violently spewing snow to the sides. He reached over and flicked on the car's red and amber lights, then climbed out, pulling up his coat zipper and fumbling with his gloves in the process.

Mike struggled around the car to his side and they waited together as the huge plow approached. The car lights and plow lights blinked in unison, then slightly out of time as if greeting one another as the driver slowed the big machine and ground to a halt beside them.

The patrolmen edged their way around the front of the giant curved blade and shook hands with the driver as he climbed down. "How far up you think we'll have to go?" he shouted, eyeing the big drift in front of them. "It's getting tougher to see the road, and I don't want to get caught too far out of town if it gets any worse."

"I don't know," Rollie shouted back. "Could be in the next mile or it could be twenty miles up the road—maybe farther."

"It ain't gonna be no farther than that," the driver hollered in return. "We've been working the main roads in sections, and the plow outa Rand has already taken Highway 34 out to about twenty miles south of here! He didn't report no stalls out to there, especially no damn big trucks."

"Well, in that case, we should be finding him soon and get back in plenty of time," Rollie answered. "How fast can that thing go?"

"Plenty! Been moving along about thirty now. Why?"

"Well, if he's within the next five or ten miles or

so, then we should be able get him and head in before the road drifts back over. As long as we stay behind you, we should make fairly good time. We'll get back early."

The driver grinned and nodded, gave a quick wave, and started climbing back into his truck. Rollie and Mike hurried to the car to avoid the wind and line up behind him. The plow's engine roared as the driver advanced, and the patrolmen watched with admiration as he crashed into the big drift and notched a gateway on through.

"Wow! Wouldn't hurt to carry one of those on the front of the car, huh?" Mike said as Rollie swung in behind.

Rollie kept the car tight on the plow's rear, focusing on the amber lights and paying little attention to the road or the ditches. The powder swirling off the truck nearly obliterated any view he would have had, anyway, so he put his trust in the driver and steered.

They progressed nearly seven miles before the plow suddenly slowed. Rollie frantically pumped the brakes to avoid sliding headfirst into its rear end, then geared down and finally stopped. The driver leaned out his cab and waved them ahead. They climbed out and struggled forward in unison, battling to reach the plow's side.

"It's there—just ahead!" The driver shouted, pointing over the top of the blade. "Looks like he slid right on off into the ditch. You want me to move up beside him?"

"Yes!" Rollie shouted, motioning at the same

time. He could barely hear the driver over the wind and engine noise and was afraid the driver couldn't hear him at all while standing directly over the plow's big power plant. The driver waved acknowledgement and got back inside. Revving the engine, he immediately pulled ahead.

"I'll walk on; you get the car!" Mike shouted. Rollie nodded and hurried back, fighting the wind for every step. It was only a matter of seconds before the plow had reached the truck's side and slipped on past.

Rollie arrived at the truck simultaneously with his partner. There was no sign of movement inside or around the semi, which was tilted about 45 degrees into the ditch. The driver's side wheels were completely buried, and the trailer box on the same side was partly covered at its base. The snow had probably prevented the big rig from continuing farther into the ditch.

"What do you think?" Mike shouted as Rollie reached his side. They stared at the cab together. Although the passenger side wheels had not left the ground, the cab was elevated higher than normal and climbing up to reach the door would be difficult.

"Check the other side first!" Rollie ordered.

Mike worked his way around the front into the deep snow. He returned quickly, shaking his head.

"Okay," Rollie said, "so we'll work on this one. "Here," he grunted, signaling with his hand at the same time, "give me a hand up here." He pointed toward the truck cab's footstep, now more than five feet above the ground.

The plow driver joined them, his face wrapped tightly in a huge wool scarf and an old-fashioned navigator's hat with woolen lining pulled down over his ears. Together, he and Mike grabbed Rollie's legs and hoisted him up.

Rollie fought for a handhold, finally reached a steel rail just behind the door, and pulled himself up. The footstep was icy and he nearly slipped off as the wind gusted around him. Watching his feet carefully, he finally anchored the left one near the cab's wall, then checked the door handle. It was frozen solid. A thick coat of ice covered the entire door.

Rollie beat on the iced-over window with his gloved fist. No response. He tried the door-release button on the handle. It was frozen tight. Leaning back to the side, he swung at the button, falling partly forward in the effort and again nearly slipping from the step. He regained his balance, then checked the button. It was still jammed solid.

"Hey!" he yelled down. Both men were watching him intently. "Get the hammer from the trunk!"

Mike careened back to the car, fighting first against the few feet of deep snow, then taking on the wind across the cleared stretch. He fumbled with the keys, got the trunk open, then let the wind push him back to the truck, carrying a claw hammer in his hand. Rollie knelt carefully and took it, getting a fresh grip on the steel rail before firmly grasping the hammer. He zeroed in on the button and smashed it with the hammer. It gave.

Once again he knelt on the step and handed back

the hammer. Standing, he grasped the door handle, depressed the button and pulled. It gave a little but remained sealed. He regripped, checked his anchor foot, and moved the right one back as a lever. Then, leaning in, he jerked backward with all his strength. The door made a cracking sound as it broke from the icy sheath. Then it snapped open. Rollie fought against falling, lost his balance, and fell backward, knocking the plow driver down and dropping face first into the snow as he rolled.

"Rollie! You okay?" Mike knelt beside him.

"Yeah, I'm fine! What about the driver?" Mike shrugged and went to the driver's side as Rollie stood and brushed the snow from his face and neck. He stared up at the door being whipped back by the wind. It crashed shut and part of the ice fell away from the window.

"How you doing?" Rollie yelled as Mike helped the driver to his feet.

"Fine!" the driver shouted back. "I've got so damn many clothes on I think a building could fall on me and not do any damage!" He laughed and brushed away some snow. Rollie slapped him on the shoulder, then pointed up to the door again. "Better get me on up again! This time I should be able to get inside!"

Mike and the driver hoisted him, and this time he pulled the door open easily and edged inside. The door banged shut behind him.

It was nearly dark inside. The thickly iced windows were letting in some light, but the change from the bright snow to the gray light stopped

Rollie for several seconds as he refocused. The seat was empty, but a quick look over the shoulder showed the wrapped form of the driver in the sleeping compartment.

"Hey, buddy, come on. You okay?" Rollie whirled around, sitting on his knees on the seat and shaking the form as he talked. The driver was unconscious. Rollie moved to his head, pulled a light blanket away, and rolled the driver toward him. Only then did he see the second form—a young girl. She, too, was unconscious. Rollie jerked off a glove and felt for the man's pulse. It was there. Then he checked the girl's. "Good," he muttered to himself. They were both alive, but their skin felt icy.

"Mike!" He shoved the door open and shouted down.

Both men looked up at his call. They had huddled closer to the cab and were stamping their feet while waiting.

"I need your help! Hurry!" He forced his weight against the door to hold it open, then placed a foot on the step and held his arm for Mike to grasp. With the plow driver pushing, Rollie pulled his partner up. He leaned back inside out of the wind as Mike established his position on the step.

"The driver's in here, and a little girl, too," Rollie puffed as they both got inside. "Back here in the sleeping compartment. They're both out, but I got a pulse."

Working together, they pulled the driver down onto the seat beside them. He moaned softly but remained unconscious.

"Let's get him out to the car, then come back for the girl."

Rollie nodded agreement to Mike's suggestion and they pulled the driver back to the edge of the seat by the door. "I'll climb down," Mike said, "and you work his body out to me."

"Okay, but try to hang on to that door, willya?"

"Yeah, I'll try," Mike said, forcing open the door. He climbed out and jumped down. The door came back shut with a bang, pummeled by a blast of wind. Rollie worked his way past the driver and reopened it. Mike stretched to hold the corner and keep it from slamming again.

The driver was big, more than six feet and 200 pounds. Rollie struggled with the man's limp body, grunting and shoving him off the edge of the seat till his legs hung out the door. Rollie eyed the door warily. If the wind ripped it away from Mike now, the door could crush the driver's legs.

He moved to place his own body against the door, then worked on pulling the driver down. Mike and the plow driver reached the man's feet and began pulling.

Holding the door open now became Rollie's responsibility. "You got him okay?" Rollie shouted, getting a foot back on the step and bracing himself. He still had one hand under the driver's left arm, trying to ease him down.

"Yes! Let him go!" Mike responded.

Rollie quickly complied. He had actually broken into a sweat working to move the unconscious man. "You want me down there?"

Mike waved him off, signaling back at the cab to indicate the girl. Rollie ducked inside. The girl looked and felt tiny compared to the driver as Rollie pulled her gently from the compartment. She was about eight or nine years old and lightly dressed. Rollie checked her breathing and pulse again. Both were shallow. She lay limply in the crook of his arm as he moved her to the door. Propping it open, he stared out at the storm. Mike and the plowman were just reaching the patrol car. He pulled the cab door shut and waited. About five minutes passed before he heard Mike's shout. Rollie pushed open the door.

"You ready? I'll hand her down!"

Mike waved. He was by himself. Rollie forced the door wider and slipped the girl out. This time there was no struggle. Mike had her almost immediately.

Rollie pulled the door shut again and looked around the cab. Grabbing the light blanket from the sleeping compartment, he locked the driver's side and pulled the keys from the ignition. He snapped the passenger-side lock and once again went through the process of forcing his way out against the raging wind. Once out on the step, he depressed the button and locked the door. Crumpling the blanket under his arm, he leaped into the snow and hurried toward the car.

"How they doin'?" he gasped, stopping by the car door. Mike was in the front seat with the little girl, while the plowman was chafing the driver's arms and legs in the back.

"The girl's hurting," Mike said worriedly. "She's so little, and so cold . . . I don't know. That driver seems to be coming around."

"You got anything hot in that plow?" Rollie directed the question to the plowman.

"Coffee," he answered, looking up momentarily. He shook his arms.

"Go get some for him," Rollie answered. "I'll work on his circulation."

"Okay, thanks," he said wearily. The layers of clothing had been hampering his movements. He backed out of the door and headed for the plow while Rollie took his place.

The driver moaned and his eyelids flickered. Rollie slapped him lightly on the cheek trying to get another response. "Where?" His eyes flickered open as he spoke and he moaned again and tried to sit up.

"Good," Rollie said with satisfaction. "Don't worry. You're in a patrol car. We found you in your truck. You've been unconscious. We'll have something hot for you to drink in a minute." He patted the man on the shoulder, then went back to chafing his legs.

"The girl. Where's the girl?" The driver sat up straighter, a panicky look on his face. Then he saw Mike in the front and leaned forward. "God!" He sank back against the seat.

"She yours?" Rollie asked.

"No, I never seen her before this morning. She's the reason I went off into the ditch."

"What?" Mike looked up questioningly.

"Yeah. I had to swerve to avoid their car back there." He waved up the road. "Must've hit a drift or something and stalled. Anyway, with the snow blowing around like it was, I didn't see the damn car till I was almost on top of it. When I swerved away, then tried to bring it back, I lost control. That's when I slid off into the ditch. Jarred the hell outa my engine too—stopped it cold. I couldn't get the damn thing to turn over, and the CB went dead, too."

"And the girl was in the car?"

"Yeah, in that car, all by herself. I don't know how long she'd been there like that, but that was about eight or so, maybe a little before. I went stormin' back there to chew that guy's butt for not setting out some kinda flares or something, but when I got there, there was just this little girl."

"Did she say anything? I mean, why she was alone there or what happened?"

"She was already out when I got there. The car was runnin' too and real warm inside. Musta been the exhaust fumes got her."

Rollie and Mike exchanged glances. It happened all the time in snow stalls, especially if the exhaust pipe got clogged. They had seen carbon monoxide deaths before.

"Anyhow, I picked her up and got her back to my truck," the driver continued. "Had one hell of a time getting her into the cab, but I figured we was safer there than anywhere else. I tried to keep her warm by wrapping us up together in the sleeping cab. I was doin' okay for a while, but then it started getting really cold in there, too. I don't remember much except being really cold. Then I guess I fell asleep. You think she'll be okay?" He leaned forward and stared at the girl's limp form. Her breathing sounded slightly strangled.

"She's fighting," Mike answered. "Rollie, we better get her to the hospital as soon as possible. Maybe we can get an ambulance out to meet us. That way the medics can get to work on her."

"Good idea. I'll call it in," Rollie said, slapping the driver on the knee and crawling outside. "You keep working on your circulation," he told the driver, "and here's your man with the coffee."

The plowman slid into the back with the driver and pulled a thermos from beneath his coat. The driver drank gratefully of the steaming liquid as Rollie got in behind the wheel and called in their situation.

"I wonder if whoever was with her made it out?" he mused, watching for a few seconds as Mike chafed the girl's arms and legs.

"I don't know, but we can't take the time to find out. If we don't get moving, she won't make it out herself."

Rollie nodded. "Can you get turned around okay?" He looked over his shoulder at the plowman.

"Yeah, I'll get it around right away." He exited lumbrously and waddled back toward the plow.

"What about my rig?" the driver asked, wiping at the back window to peer at his truck.

"Here's the keys," Rollie replied, handing them over the seat. "I locked it up. You can bring a tow back out after the storm lets up. We haven't got any way or enough time to get it out now."

Rollie shifted and began pulling the car around. The snow impeded his efforts, but after several minutes he was facing back into the wind. He pulled as far to one side as possible to let the plow pass. The plow driver, too, had to work to get his machine turned back, but several minutes later, he succeeded and pulled alongside.

"Take it as fast as possible but keep us in your mirror!" Rollie shouted from the window. "If we're having any problems, we'll stop, and we don't want to lose you!"

The driver waved acknowledgement and pulled ahead, quickly picking up speed and keeping the plow blade down. It had been almost an hour since they'd arrived at the truck and already several new drifts had formed over the highway.

Rollie settled in behind the wheel, while Mike wrapped the girl tightly in the light blanket and held her close to keep her warm. The driver sat quietly in back, grasping a second cup of coffee with both hands. He was shaking spasmodically.

"Whoa!" Rollie cried suddenly, rapidly pumping at the brakes as a dark object blew up from the ditch directly into his path. He brought the car to a near halt as a large chunk of cardboard went whirling over the hood. He stared past Mike, watching it into the other ditch, then started to step down on the footfeed again.

The plow had slowed to wait.

As he swung his gaze back to concentrate on the road, another dark object caught the corner of his eye. "Whoa again," he said softly. Mike looked at him curiously as Rollie pulled the car to a complete stop and backed up. "There," he pointed over Mike's shoulder. "I think. . . ."

"Jesus Christ," Mike said, carefully placing the wrapped girl's body on the seat beside him.

Rollie was already out of the car and sprinting around the front, one hand on the hood to stabilize himself against the icy road. Mike forgot about his gloves as he jumped out, ordering the driver to stay put. Rollie already was at the road's edge kneeling over the object.

Mike stopped at Rollie's shoulder and dropped on his knees beside him.

"Well, now we know why she was there alone," Rollie said.

"Yeah," Mike answered. "Now we know."

Together they began pulling a man's frozen body from the ditch to carry him to the car. His only clothing was a light wool dress suit; on his feet were ordinary, low-cut street shoes.

CHAPTER EIGHT

"Jesus, lady, I wish you could have picked another day to have your baby! It's really bad out here!" Lorre fought the wheel as the truck plowed into another big drift and the pain shot through his left side again. He gritted his teeth and tried to ignore it, straining to see the road through the blowing snow and cracked windshield.

"Well, at least the heater works in this thing." He tried to sound cheerful as he glanced at Jean's face. She started to smile back, but a contortion of pain eliminated it. "How you doin'?" he asked.

"I'm—I'm okay," Jean replied. "It hurts, you know, a lot, and well . . . well, it hurts."

Lorre was silent, concentrating on the road. He cursed as the wind buffeted the old truck, nearly pushing them into the ditch. "Damnit, aren't there any hardtop roads around here?" The gravel was pitted with chuckholes and each caused him to slide sideways as he hit it.

"Ye-yes," Jean said, trying to see through the windshield. "We should have reached one by now. It's the main road running east and west. You'll have to turn right to head west into Marion."

Lorre looked at her in surprise. "Right? You mean left. If we go right, we'll be heading east."

"No-no, it's right . . ." she paused. "You did turn right from our driveway, didn't you?"

"No. I went left. Sonofabitch." He drove on silently, contemplating their options. "Are there any main roads at all this way that go west?"

"No—yes—uh—well, I'm not so sure," she hesitated as she thought it over. "Well, there's a real good gravel road somewhere up here that runs east and west. We could try that. If it doesn't go into Marion, at least it runs past some farms . . . I think." She looked helplessly at the big man behind the wheel. "I'm sorry, I-I should have told you to go right."

"Don't worry about it," he said gruffly, trying to avoid her look. "You just hang in there and we'll make it." He concentrated on the wheel. "Once I get you there safe, you're on your own, you know. I don't want no lawman grabbing me while I'm trying to get you to a doctor or to some house. No way!" He looked over at Jean, but she looked so miserable, sitting there clutching at her stomach, that he decided not to push it.

"The pain's getting worse," she said. "Hope we can find something soon."

"I'm sure we . . . goddamn," he swore as he nearly lost the wheel when the tires hit a hole and started sliding. Pulling the truck back on line, he sighed in relief. It was a good thing it was still light, he thought. There would be no way to control the truck and keep it on the road after dark.

They were moving a lot slower now as they bucked through bigger drifts. The truck's high clearance was paying off, Lorre thought. Probably the only thing keeping them from getting stuck. Suddenly, a stop sign appeared through the snow.

"Aren't you going to stop?" Jean asked, her voice displaying concern as Lorre plowed past the sign and turned west onto a larger gravel road.

Lorre looked at her with amazement, then burst into laughter, almost losing the truck into the passenger-side ditch in the process. "Jesus, lady, you know you take the prize. We're fighting one of the worst snow storms I've ever seen, you're about to have a baby in the middle of it, and you're worried about me not stopping at a crummy stop sign on a deserted road."

He shook his head slowly, then laughed again.

"What?" Jean looked at him quizzically.

"I was just thinking how damn funny it would be if I were picked up now for running that stop sign." He laughed at the thought and Jean joined in. It was the first genuine laugh he'd heard from her since they'd met.

"Do you think this is that road?" He was relaxing a little. Although the snow was still drifted, this road was wider and less pitted. He had more room to maneuver the old truck.

"I think so." She leaned forward to confirm it, then sat back.

"Hey, lady, what's your name anyway?"

"Jean."

Lorre nodded. "Well, I'd say nice to meetya, but under the circumstances, I guess I'll keep my big mouth shut."

Jean laughed again, then looked toward him sympathetically.

"Thank you . . . for helping me. I didn't mean for you and your partner to fight like that, but thank you."

He nodded, growing solemn as he thought of the battle.

"You're . . . " she held back a second, "you're the convicts, aren't you? You're the ones who escaped from the State Prison last night?"

Lorre looked at her carefully, then nodded. "Yes."

"I heard . . . they said a man was killed . . . that you killed a man."

"A man was killed," Lorre said, not looking at her. "I'm not covering for myself, but it was that crazy Schumacher did it. I don't know what the hell's gotten into him, or why he's done any of the things he's been doing since we made our break. He just did it. I guess it's my fault, too. But, lady," he added, turning to look at Jean, "I wouldn't kill nobody . . . at least not on purpose."

"But why did you escape?" Jean grimaced as she asked the question, and Lorre could see she was having another pain. "I mean, you must know they'll catch you again, or even worse. And now you'll miss a chance for parole or something like that, won't you?"

"Parole," Lorre laughed bitterly. "Yeah, parole, I guess so. But it was a long time comin' for me yet, and I couldn't stand to wait no longer. I'm a free-spirit type, you know what I mean? I love the out-doors and the fresh air, and just plain ol' places. Hell, I can't even stand to be cooped up in a small room for too long. I need . . ." he paused to emphasize his point, "I *need* to be free."

He stared silently at the road for a few seconds, then spoke again. "Everyday I was in that place it was like spending a day in hell. Oh, the people didn't always treat me so bad, but it was still things, you know. Things I had to do just 'cause they said so. And then getting locked in that cell at night. Oh, God!" He shuddered involuntarily. "When that door snapped shut, it was like they shut off all the fresh air and put me in a box. You ever get the feeling you're suffocating? Well, I got that feeling every night for *three* years. Finally, I just had to get out. One way or another, I had to get out."

He stopped talking to curse again at the snow and swerve the old truck back more toward the road's center. They had now gone two miles on this road and he had yet to see any other sign of life besides themselves. He shivered as a stronger blast of icy wind rocked the truck.

"Lorre, why were you in prison?" Jean asked the question timidly but looked at him steadily as if demanding a response.

112

He hesitated for a few seconds, then answered. "It was a mistake. Just a mistake." He drove on, not speaking, then began relating the story as if prompted.

"We'd been at work all day, me'n some buddies, and we stopped at the bar for just a couple to wash down the dust. Well, it started out real friendly, but as it got later and later, some of us got liquored up real bad. I guess some of the guys got edgy. Anyway, I mentioned something about this John Lancer's girl. I only meant it in fun, but he got real uptight and called me out.

"So we went out, me'n John and a bunch of drunks. Hell, I had John by twenty, maybe thirty pounds, so it really wasn't much of a fight. Anyway, no one bothered pullin' us apart—just stood by drinkin' and laughin' and watchin'. I guess I hit him real hard and he fell against the side of the brick building. I quick jumped over and grabbed him by the shirt, jerkin' him up on his feet. Only . . . only he was out. I mean really out. So, I just let him drop back down again and went inside. Poor old John, he never came to, and all those boys with me could remember was me knockin' John against the wall, then jerkin' him up again. Some of 'em swore I beat his head against the wall. Maybe I did. Hell, I was drunk.

"They called it second-degree murder. Well, my lawyer—he was given to me by the state—he said I should plead guilty to third-degree and he'd get me a light sentence. So, I did what he said. The judge gave me twenty years." He paused. "That man Lancer died, Jean. He died, but I didn't murder him!" He looked at her face to see if she understood what he was saying. "It was a stupid thing, a mistake, fighting like that when we were drunk, but that was it, a mistake. They said I killed him with my fists. Beat him to death. Even drunk I wouldn't beat a man to death. I love life too much. I could never take it from someone else."

He emitted a long sigh. Jean sat staring at him, not saying anything. "Prison . . . it, it was a real bad scene, you know. I thought at first I could hang on till parole came up, but it wasn't no use. So, we decided to escape. Me'n Jack back there and Bill—he was shot when we made our break. I thought they were like me, you know, just not able to stand bein' cooped up anymore. I guess I read Jack all wrong. He was in for murder and that's probably what he done. All that time in that hole and I got to callin' him my best friend."

He stopped and coughed. "Best friend. I guess I just blocked it out of my mind, the chance of him bein' guilty. He just seemed to be the only one who really understood me and the way I felt about bein' locked up. Do you know what I mean, lady—uh, Jean? Have you ever wanted a friend so bad you just couldn't think any bad things about him, no matter what? Well, I guess that's the way it was with me and Jack."

"I'm sorry—mostly for you," Jean said as she watched him contend with another snow drift. "But now . . . well . . . you know they'll find you. They always do. Then you'll have to go back, and probably for longer than before. What then?"

"There's not going to be a problem there, because I'm not going back. If I have to die to stay free, then I guess I will 'cause I wasn't meant to stay in that cage. If they're going to capture me, then I'll fight them till I'm dead. Don't worry, I won't go back. Anyway, let's not worry about things like that. Right now all I'm worried about is seein' you get to that doctor."

He shivered again, then strained to see through the increasingly bad gusts of snow blocking his view. The road outlines were becoming harder to follow.

"Do you think you'll be able to drive on like this?" Jean asked, as he fought against the storm.

"I don't know, but I'm tryin'. The truck is sittin' up real high, so we're going on through the snow real good. If I don't slide too much, we'll be okay. I used to drive one like this back on our home place near Hampstead. You know where that's at?"

"Yes, I know it well," Jean said, surprise in her tone. "We lived over in that corner of the state, too, for a while, earlier, when Rollie first started."

"Yeah? It's a nice place. We had a couple acres outside of town." Lorre smiled at the memory.

"Yes, we enjoyed it, too," she answered.

He looked at her again. She seemed to be relaxing more, less frightened of him than before. He smiled.

"Does your family still live there?"

Lorre's face clouded and he slowly shook his head. "No. There ain't no one left now. It was just the three of us. Mom died when I was eighteen, and Dad

. . ." his voice caught briefly. "Dad, he just, well, he just gave up when I . . . when I got put in prison. He came to visit me for a while and I could see he was lookin' pretty bad. Then they told me he was sick . . ." he paused again. "He died about a year ago."

Jean bowed her head, then reached over and touched his arm. "I'm sorry," she said softly.

"Oh, that's okay," he answered. "Thanks, anyway."

She nodded and they rode on in silence. They were moving progressively slower, but Lorre was keeping the speedometer on or near the twenty-miles-per-hour mark. As the wind howled around them, he broke the silence.

"It's weird, this weather. Hell, I can remember taking a day this time of year to go hunting or fishing back home. Now look at this, snowing like crazy. It's really weird, don't you think?"

He looked to her for her answer, but she wasn't nodding. Instead, she was doubling over and gasping heavily. "Hey! You gonna make it okay?" He reached over to put a hand on her shoulder, forgetting his own pain.

She shook her head no. "It-it's the baby. I think it's time!"

"Oh, Christ!" Lorre panicked. "Jean, come on, you've got to hold on! There's no room in here, and besides, I don't know one damn thing about how to help you. Hang on, okay?" He stepped down on the footfeed to speed up the old truck, but it immediately started side-slipping in response and he plowed into the biggest drift they had tried.

116

The motor sputtered as the powder enveloped them. Then it stalled. He grabbed at the key and ground the motor. No response. "Oh, hell!" Lorre looked at Jean with exasperation. She gasped again and he turned his attention back to the dash, glaring at it wild-eyed.

"Come on, you bastard, start!"

He turned the key over again, but the motor just rasped and whirred, still not firing. Lorre looked over toward her. "I don't know what to do," he said. "We might be stuck here. I can't get it to start. Damn! It's my damn rotten luck as usual."

"There must be . . . something," Jean cried. "Maybe under the hood."

Lorre leaped out into the snow. Fighting the hood latch, he finally jerked it open and lifted it. Snow was packed in around the motor. He brushed at it quickly, then slammed his open right hand down on the air cleaner. More snow dropped away. "Hell," he said in frustration, "I don't know what to do." He slammed the hood back down and got inside.

It was already cooling off in the cab. They could freeze to death sitting in this thing, he thought. "Goddamnit, start!" he commanded the truck, then mashed the key over again. The engine whirred, then began grinding down, barely turning. The battery was losing power. He started to let it up when it sputtered.

"Come on, baby, come on," he coaxed, pumping the footfeed quickly, trying to keep the spark alive. It chugged and wheezed in response, backfired, then caught. Lorre held the footfeed to the floor, roaring the engine for several seconds. "Now . . . let's see if this thing'll go," he said, shifting back into gear.

"Hurry," Jean said weakly. Her face urged him more than her voice.

Lorre eased the truck forward. For several seconds it did not move. The wheels seemed suspended, caught on top of the snow and spinning. Then it rattled ahead, picked up some speed and advanced. Lorre resumed the steady pace he had been holding before.

Jean began rocking, quietly moaning "Oh God, oh God," over and over. Lorre tried not to look her way. Seeing her pain just enhanced the throbbing pain of his own, now pulsing through the entire left side of his body.

"Hey! Look!" He cried jubilantly. Jean tried to look up from her doubled-over position.

"It's a farm! Maybe my luck's finally starting to change! I'll get you there in no time. What a break!" He forgot his shoulder and slapped the steering wheel with his left hand. The pain shot through his body, quickly cooling his jubilation.

He negotiated the driveway entrance and slowed as the buildings took shape. The truck shuddered as the snow deepened. He shifted to keep the motor from killing. He was nearly halfway up the drive. Suddenly, the back wheels slid sideways and the right one dropped. The engine shuddered again, then died.

"Goddamnit!" Lorre fumed as he turned over the key. It started, but refused to budge. Shoving open the door, he hurried to the rear end. The right wheel

118

was buried in a hole along the driveway's edge. "Damn, damn!" He cursed and struggled up the right side, pulling open the passenger door.

"Come on," he motioned with his head. "We'll walk to the farm." His words were drowned by the wind, but Jean nodded acknowledgement. He helped her out, but she only took two steps in the deep snow before she stopped.

Lorre looked at his shoulder. It was still throbbing, but the bleeding seemed to have stopped. "Oh, hell," he said aloud, "what's the choice?" He leaned forward to maintain his balance, then reached down and picked her up. He fought back tears from his searing shoulder.

The walk, although only about seventy-five yards, was one of the longest and most painful he could remember making. Twice he nearly fell, each time sending waves of pain through his body. The shoulder was bleeding freely again before they had gone halfway. The snow was blinding him and Jean kept her face buried against his chest. He wanted to stop but knew he didn't dare, more for her sake than his.

The first of the buildings was coming up. They reached the corner of what he thought must be a barn and stepped in along side. Immediately, the wind was checked from the break. Leaning against the side for support, he put Jean down in the snow, then fought to regain his breath. "Look, you stay here," he puffed, "and I'll go on to the house to get help."

Jean nodded. Lorre stepped back into the icy

blast, shielding his eyes in the process. He studied the farmstead but could only see snow, then he cupped both hands over his eyes to block out some of the whiteness. Now he could see the outlines of the other buildings, set up in a horseshoe-shaped fashion. He paused, took two steps to his right, then kicked at the snow violently. "Oh, no! Dear God, no!"

He turned his back to the wind and blinked away tears of frustration. He had scanned the farm buildings thoroughly. Where the house had stood, only a foundation remained. The farm had been abandoned.

CHAPTER NINE

"All units, this is Zebra base, over." The radio rasped out the message, punctuated with static at every word.

Rollie pulled the mike free to respond. "This is Zebra Nine." The other cars followed in a general call-in.

"All units, you are now advised to return to base at earliest possible due to the storm's intensity. If you have a definite lead or call, please advise."

Rollie grunted and snapped the mike back on the hook, hitting the squelch button to cut down some of the static. He shifted to get more comfortable and glanced at his watch. Two-thirty. It would be a half hour back to the base, then he'd call Jean. He sighed. Nine hours without a break. He was exhausted.

Mike negotiated a corner and turned the car back home. "Christ! This is ridiculous!" He said it more to himself than to Rollie, but Rollie nodded agreement just the same. The snow made visibility just about nil and he was developing a headache from the constant strain of watching the road.

"You kinda have to feel sorry for those poor bastards, don'tcha?"

Mike's voice pulled Rollie from his thoughts. "What poor bastards?"

"Those escaped cons. Jesus, can you imagine being caught out in this? Not me! Wonder if they found that ambulance yet?"

"Don't know, but I heard a couple of guys at the hospital talking about a motorist's report of an accident up north. They said it involved an ambulance or something like that. Maybe that was part of this whole escape business. You think?"

Mike shrugged and struggled momentarily with the wheel as the car skidded.

"Sounded like they had a pretty stupid plan," Rollie continued. "God, can you imagine just trying to drive away from that place? You've either got to have one hell of a lot of confidence in yourself or not too much upstairs."

"Yeah, well, when they find their frozen bodies, I think the ruling will be for the latter," Mike responded. "It's really a sonofabitch out here!"

"How much snow you think we've got?"

"I don't know, but I don't ever remember getting so much so early in the year. The last time you were out, the desk reported eight-ten more inches had fallen. Ever hear of so much by now?"

"No," Rollie answered, rolling his window

partway down to check the roadside build-up. The snow swirled into the car, but he left the window down. He was worried about Jean. But hell, he rationalized with himself, why worry? Even if she's snowed in, the furnace is ready and there's a good supply of food. At the latest, it would only be a day or so before he could get home.

They sat in silence as Mike gingerly guided the car home. Rollie's sigh was echoed by Mike's when they finally reached the station. Several other cars were arriving from the call-in and Mike pulled to a stop to let one pass ahead of him.

"Hey, look, can you check the car in okay? I'd like to run in and phone Jean. I guess I'm just a worrier." Rollie looked anxiously at his partner and Mike waved him on.

"But you better name the kid after me!" He exclaimed as Rollie started to shut the door.

"Yeah, I can see it now," Rollie answered. "Hens Patterson. She'll be the talk of the town."

Mike gunned the car toward the motor pool as Rollie jogged to the main building, stomped snow from his shoes, and walked in. Several patrolmen were already inside, some sipping coffee and quietly talking. The radio crackled loudly over their noise.

Rollie returned a wave to a couple of the patrolmen, then walked straight to the desk where Sergeant Granzetti was on the phone. He waited patiently until the sergeant had finished his conversation.

"Well, Patterson, what can I do for you?" He hardly glanced up from the papers he was working on as he asked the question. His face was drawn and he looked tired from the day's strain.

"Two things, Sarge. Do you have a road report for my part of the country, and can I use this phone to call home?"

"No and yes. But I'll see what I can find out on the first half while you call." He gave Rollie a tired smile, then pushed the phone toward him and got up to check with the radio dispatcher.

Rollie smiled back his thanks, then eagerly grabbed the receiver and pulled the phone around to face him. He dialed quickly but was greeted by a busy signal. He looked at his watch. *Now* who'd be calling? Maybe Jean was trying to call here. He dialed again. Still busy.

With a perplexed expression on his face, he put the receiver down and walked over to the coffee machine. Extracting a cup, he gulped some down as he walked back to the desk, burning his tongue in the process. He cursed at himself, then dialed again. Busy. God, he was tired. He sipped the coffee slowly, forgetting about the burn.

The sergeant came back, held up a finger to wait and took another call. "It looks like the roads out your way are in tough shape," he said, putting the phone down. "Traffic control reports pulling several cars out of drifts or the ditch in that sector, and the snow seems to be heavier there, moving this way. Did you get through to your wife?"

"No," Rollie answered, feeling panicky for the first time. "My wife's in her eighth month. I'd sure hate to have something happen and. . . ."

Granzetti cut him off. "Look, just call again, then if you still can't get through we'll see if there's a problem. Okay?"

Rollie nodded and redialed. The line was still busy. He put the receiver on the desk top, then picked it back up and dialed the operator. She promised to check and call back. He stood uneasily, finishing the coffee and checking his watch again. Three-fifteen.

The phone rang and the sergeant firmly took it from his hand before Rollie could answer. Granzetti nodded, saying, "I see, um-hmmm, yes, okay, thanks." He hung up. "Well, seems like some of the power lines are down and some telephone lines are iced up, too. Operator says there's a good chance a lot of the phones there will be out for a day or so. Do you think your wife's in any danger?"

"N-no, I mean, well I don't think so. I guess I'm being a little over-cautious, you know, this being our first baby and all, and her so far from any help. Do you think there's any way of my getting home?"

"Let me check." Granzetti picked up the phone again and rapidly made two calls, then a third, before returning his attention to Rollie. "Now, here's what I've got set up. We'll need a plow to get you through, but most of them'll be tied up for at least a couple hours, particularly in and around town. They've got to keep the city streets cleared to keep traffic moving. Once that rush is over, they'll be able to concentrate on emergencies. You'll get a plow then. So, all I can say is sit tight, get yourself some chow and try not to worry. I'm sure your wife is fine." He smiled, his voice sounded reassuring.

Rollie faintly smiled back. "Yeah, okay, Sarge, thanks for your help. Look, uh, I'll be in the patrol lounge. You'll let me know the first minute things are ready, huh?"

Granzetti nodded and waved him away, then turned back to his paperwork, stopping to answer the phone once again. Rollie walked to the door. His stomach felt queazy. Mike stomped in just as he reached the doorway.

"Hey, what's happening, man? You look sick or something. Anything wrong?" Henson put an arm on Rollie's shoulder as he spoke. "You okay?"

Rollie looked up. "Huh? Oh, yeah. I'm fine. Just a little nervous I guess. Can't get through to Jean and there's no way to be heading home for several hours either. Sure hope nothing's wrong!"

"Hey, come on. Jean's not stupid and she's capable of taking care of herself, storm or no storm, right?"

"Well, I guess I'm more worried about the baby being so close."

"So close!" Mike cut in quickly. "Why, there's a good month to go yet. And didn't you tell me that after you two took those classes you could probably deliver the baby yourself if you had to? Don't you think Jean knows what's going on?"

"Yeah, I guess." Rollie leaned against the window sill and stared out at the storm, then he started to rationalize again. "Yeah, and besides, I guess if to-day was going to be the day, she would've been hav-

126

ing pains this morning, don't you think?"

Mike slapped him on the back. "Sure, don't worry. Now come on, let's get something to eat and then we'll worry about your getting home later. We've still got reports to fill out."

Rollie nodded and zipped up his jacket as they went outside. The diner was across the street from the base. They ate slowly, working on the form reports to help use up the time. It was nearly five when they returned to headquarters. Both men flopped down on the soft chairs in the patrolmen's lounge, then Mike jumped up again. "How 'bout some coffee and a look at the paper?"

Rollie mumbled an okay, then slipped off his jacket, balling it up behind him for a cushion. Mike tossed the paper delivery-boy style across the room and Rollie opened it to read the bold headlines about the prison break. A late-breaking supplement revealed that the ambulance had still not been located, although a motorist had reported something resembling it pulled off into the trees on a dirt road near Hollysberg. The story did not say which side of town the possible ambulance sighting had been made.

Mike returned, juggling the coffee cups as he gingerly placed one foot before the other.

"You know, this story says the ambulance may have been spotted near here. Did any of the guys get a chance to check it?" Rollie asked.

"Nope, the snow was too heavy. That sighting was made somewhere out northwest. Say, isn't that the direction to your place?"

127

"Yeah, west," Rollie answered, taking one of the cups. He stared glumly at the words, not reading.

"Aw, will you quit worrying?" Mike said, looking at Rollie's face. "There's probably one chance in a million those guys even headed in the direction of your place. Jesus, talk about the eternal pessimist, you've sure as hell been acting like one today. Besides, with the snow so bad, they're either frozen, like I said before, or they're holed up in some shack somewhere waiting out the storm. Now relax, willya?"

Rollie stared back at the paper in response, rereading the part about the ambulance sighting and trying to pick out dirt roads in the vicinity of his home in his mind. Finally, he shook his head and looked up at his partner. "Hey, why are you still hanging around? All our reports are completed."

"I just thought I'd hang in here to see what happens with you getting home. I want to make sure everything's going to be okay, ya know, in case that plow don't get through for you." He added hurriedly, "you'll need a place to stay if that happens, right?"

Rollie smiled at Mike's cover-up tactics. "Sure. Okay, thanks."

Mike turned his back and stretched, signifying the subject was closed. Rollie smiled again, then tossed the paper back across the room at him. Mike picked it up, then sat down to sip at his coffee and scan the news. Rollie watched him for a few seconds, sipping at his own cup, then leaned back wearily and tried to rest. He was just starting to doze when a hand on his shoulder brought him back.

"Plow's on the way. You ready?" It was Granzetti, now bundled up and ready to head outside.

Stretching, Rollie stood and pulled on his coat. Mike was also up and rubbing his eyes.

"Why don't you go ahead and check out a patrol car?" the sergeant said, stopping by the lounge door. "It's better equipped for this than your car and you can bring it in tomorrow and pick yours up then."

Mike and Rollie nodded in unison, and Granzetti turned to go, then turned back. "Henson, what are you still doing here?"

"Oh, I thought I'd ride along out and make sure everything's okay," Mike responded. "I'll catch a ride back with the plow."

Rollie glanced at his partner as if to say something, then just smiled. He was glad he wasn't going to be following the plow on his own.

"You think there's going to be some sort of trouble?" Granzetti asked suspiciously.

"No, no, none at all," Mike said hurriedly. "But, you know, that ambulance *was* sighted out that way, and if we see those guys wandering around in the snow, I want to be there to help get them started back on the right path. Can't let this guy get all the good collars now, can I?" He winked at Granzetti, who scowled in return.

"It's okay with me, Sarge. I could use the company on the way out, if Mike doesn't mind," Rollie glanced to the sergeant for a positive response.

"Yeah, okay," he answered gruffly and walked away.

The two men walked together to the motor pool, rechecked out the car they had been driving earlier and explained to the sergeant there why they needed it and why it would be out overnight. After filling in the sign-out time at just after six, Rollie took the wheel.

The plow pulled in, lights flashing on top and sides. Rollie switched the patrol car lights on, too. It was dark now and he knew the darkness would make the driving and visibility a lot tougher on the open road. Granzetti came walking toward them, leaning into the wind with a hand on his hat as he advanced. Rollie rolled down the window as the sergeant reached the car.

"Look, I don't want you guys looking for no escaped cons tonight," he ordered. "Just get the hell home, Patterson, and then we'll see you regular time tomorrow. Hell, in the first place we don't even have a confirmed sighting on an ambulance out that way—just a motorist's report, so don't go jumping to no conclusions. That understood?"

Both men nodded and Granzetti turned to go. "Oh, by the way," he said, turning back, and ducking down out of the wind. "You guys handled that truck thing on 34, right?"

Once again they nodded in unison.

"Well, the hospital just gave us a call and that little girl—she's gonna be okay. She regained consciousness about an hour ago." The patrolmen exchanged grins at the news. "It's a hell of a thing," the sergeant added solemnly. "That was her ol' man you found frozen there and now the hospital says she doesn't have no mother alive either. They're looking around for an aunt and uncle livin' here in Hollysberg. It's a hell of a thing." He shook his head and walked away.

"I'm glad she's going to make it," Mike said, breaking a sustained silence as they watched Granzetti go, illuminated in patches by the plow's whirling light.

"Yeah, so'm I," Rollie sighed. "Too bad about her father, though. She's so young."

Mike grunted agreement. "Wonder how that sick little boy's doing?"

Rollie turned crimson thinking of the early morning debacle. He was glad it was dark in the car so Mike couldn't see his face. "I don't know," Rollie quietly replied, "I hope okay."

"Yeah, that would make the day worthwhile." Mike shifted around as he spoke. "Hey, look, man, why not let me handle this rig and you get in the plow? Didn't you tell me there were some tricky turns to your place?"

"Yeah, but Jesus, I hate to leave you behind in this thing alone."

"Don't worry," Mike answered, already sliding toward the driver's side. "You keep that rig on the road and I'll keep this one tight on your tail. Just don't slow up too quick or you'll have me smeared up your rear end. How far is it?"

"Twenty-three miles."

"Okay, so don't sit there all day, that's still a hell of a haul, and I plan to make it home tonight for supper."

Rollie smiled and slid out. Mike was already buckling himself into the driver's side.

Stepping up on the passenger side, Rollie climbed into the snow-plow cab. The driver looked at him questioningly, but said nothing, waiting for his instructions.

"I'm Officer Patterson," Rollie said simply. "We'll be heading out on 21, west. There's a couple miles back roads, too."

The driver immediately shifted and pulled out onto the highway. It appeared as if the snow had let up somewhat.

"It's letting up some now, isn't it?" Rollie said.

"Nope." The driver downshifted to turn west on Highway 21. "Just seems lighter here because of the buildings. It's still heavy in the country. Your friend planning on sticking close?"

"Yeah, he does," Rollie responded, deciding the driver was probably in no mood for any idle talk.

The streets were snowpacked, but not drifted over. As they pulled out of town, visibility suddenly dropped and the driver lowered the huge blade into position. At first, he pushed snow off to the north ditch, but the wind began whipping it back toward the windshield. Cursing, he turned the blade to the south, flinging the snow out over the other lane. "You don't see this," he said to Rollie as he worked the controls. "Don't think we'll have to worry about meeting any traffic tonight, anyway. Okay?"

Rollie sat back, saying nothing. "Look," he finally answered after the driver looked his way twice. "I don't care if you stack the damn snow down the center line as long as you get me home."

The driver nodded. Soon the only sound was the plow's whine and the constant thumps as the blade bit into drift after drift.

Behind them, Mike strained at the wheel and kept the plow's rear flashing light in view. Occasionally he would interrupt the silence surrounding him to mutter, "You damn blizzard!"

CHAPTER TEN

Lorre knelt at Jean's side. She stared inquiringly up at him, clutching at her stomach.

"There's no house. The place is abandoned!" He was scared and she could see it.

"Look, don't worry. . . ." The words came rapidly and she grasped Lorre's arm as she said them. "Let's . . . let's get in out of this cold. Get me into this barn, then we'll take things from there," she nodded at him reassuringly and gave him a faint smile. She had spoken so calmly, he relaxed a little.

Lorre helped her up and led her through the snow around the corner of the old building. The wind ripped through their clothing and blinded them with snow. Lorre found the door and pulled it open, jerking back a load of snow with it.

The light inside was poor, but they could see piles of bales and some loose hay. The barn was nearly filled with hay, and Jean pointed to a large loose stack and he helped her down onto a bale beside it.

"Help me," she said simply. Working quickly, they smoothed the stack out. In the same motion, Lorre pulled off his coat and laid it down on top.

"Okay, come on, lay down!" he said excitedly. "Jesus, I don't know what the hell to do. What do you want me to do? I don't know how to help you!" He looked at her with a trace of fear in his eyes.

She gulped as her throat suddenly seemed full of air, then she sat down on the hay. Another pain ripped through her body, then she realized her water had broken. "It's starting," she said, so calmly she almost shocked herself. "You'll have to help me now, okay?"

"I don't know if it's okay, lady. What the hell do I know about delivering a baby? I haven't even had a course in first aid." Lorre looked helpless.

"Don't worry, I'll tell you what to do. I've got to get my legs up and get these pants off. You'll have to do it." She looked at him steadily, then grimaced as contractions cascaded one after another. "And I've got to get my head up where I can see."

Lorre pushed more hay in behind her to raise her head and shoulders, then jerked at her slacks, finally getting them loose and pulling them away. Jean moved her hips and legs onto the coat, then began tugging at her underpants. Lorre hesitated, then fumbled with them at Jean's guidance. Finally, he had them over her shoes and off.

Jean was sweating heavily, even though she knew it couldn't be much more than 30 or 40 degrees in the old barn. She struggled with her coat. "Help me get this off and under me too, please!"

Lorre responded, almost automatically, at the urgency in her command. He shivered, then rubbed at his shoulder, a move which brought a grimace of pain to his face.

Jean could see he was watching her every move with intenseness. She licked her lips. "My mouth . . . it's so dry. I'm really thirsty." She looked around the barn.

"Snow," Lorre said immediately and jumped up and walked to the door. He came back with a handful of the pure-white powder and pushed it toward her. Jean put some in her mouth and moistened her lips with the rest.

Suddenly, she felt the urge to push, as if she had to push the baby out to ease the pains coursing through her body. "Never push it out. Fight the urge." She pictured the middle-aged nurse standing in front of the room at the prenatal classes admonishing the young mothers-to-be before her. "Learn to control your breathing and it'll be much, much easier," the nurse had directed.

Got to control my breathing, concentrate on it, Jean thought as she began panting and blowing out in regulation.

"What are you doing? You okay?" Lorre was panicking again, kneeling at her side.

"I'm—okay! I've got to breathe this way—to help—the baby. Got to—slow—things down," she panted the sentence out. "It'll help—the baby, and keep from tearing—me open. Now—dammit—let

136

me worry," she gulped, "about what—I'm doing! I'll tell you—what to do—when the time comes!"

Lorre nodded and moved back to her feet. He stared, transfixed, watching her work the breathing rhythm. He looked very helpless, Jean thought. A quarter hour passed; then a half. She moved her arms back and forth across her stomach, finally locking her hands tightly to keep them still.

Suddenly, Lorre started. The top of the baby's head had begun to appear. Jean continued steadily panting, and the head came through completely. Lorre sank back on his knees, moving his good arm up to hold his wounded one. He seemed to be struggling to hold back his assistance. Then she remembered her earlier admonishment to him about holding back till she directed. He stared intently at the small head, as if hypnotized by the sight of the birth's beginning. Jean nearly had to shout to break the spell.

"Now, Lorre, now! You've got to take the head. You have to support the head!" She was watching as the baby's head advanced and panting harder to prevent herself from tearing.

Lorre lurched forward and took the tiny head, supporting it clumsily. He looked frightened. Jean watched as the baby's body started through. It's unbelievable, she thought, where's the pain? She began bearing down, pushing the shoulders out with the next few contractions. Now there was some pain. Lorre continued supporting the head, never wavering as he held it.

"Now a hand—on—the shoulders!" Jean panted

as more of the body came out. Lorre shifted his grip and his hand nearly slid away as he tried to grasp the slippery body. His other hand remained firmly on the head. "Once—once the baby—is free—you've got to get the phlegm away from—from it's mouth!" Jean gasped.

"Phlegm?" Lorre looked at her, as if not understanding.

"The mucus over its face," she nearly screamed.

"Oh," he responded, returning his gaze back to the baby's head.

She watched carefully, then panting more as the rest of the baby came through. She felt enormous relief, yet worry. Lorre pulled the baby free and cautiously wiped the mucus from its face and mouth, partially opening the baby's mouth with a finger.

"Now what?" He held the baby up; it was a girl.

"Slap the baby lightly, and get her to cry." He eyed the tiny body in his hands, as if wondering how to slap it lightly, then turned it over and tapped it. The baby gasped, then cried.

Jean smiled weakly, still holding her head and shoulders up to watch his movements. "Okay, hold her head downward and try to drain out some more mucus. Lorre obeyed, looking extremely awkward with the small body in his big hands.

The cord started to get in his way as he turned the baby, and without pause, he untangled it and pushed it to one side. The baby still cried. Lorre stared, his face filled with wonder, as if finding it hard to believe he was holding her.

138

Jean smiled again broadly as she watched the big man maneuver the small body. She leaned back and breathed out a long sigh. She felt warm but was trembling. Then she laughed and cried at once.

"Oh God, it's wonderful, it's wonderful! I just can't believe it's so wonderful! Beautiful!" She laughed again. Her stomach was flipflopping, but she felt good—no, more than good—glorious! "Thank you, God, thank you! And Lorre, thank you!" She smiled again and he smiled shyly back and moved the baby toward her body.

Jean took her, then realized how cold she must be. "We've got to get the baby dry and warm. It's freezing in here!"

Lorre looked around the old barn. There was plenty of hay but little more. Without speaking, he took off his shirt. It stuck at his shoulder and bits of cloth stayed in the wound as he pulled it away. More blood trickled down his arm. Then in obvious pain, he peeled off his t-shirt and held it toward her.

Jean took it and gasped at the sight of his shattered shoulder. "My God! I had no idea you were hurt!"

"I guess I caught one of Jack's last bullets there," Lorre said matter-of-factly, glancing down at the raw, ragged tear in his shoulder. The edges of the wound were already turning blue while blood still oozed from the hole. The sleeve of his shirt was hardened with caked blood. Grimacing again, he pulled the shirt back on, then fumbled at fastening the buttons. His fingers were trembling.

"Hey! We didn't go through all that so the baby'd

freeze to death, did we? You better get her dried off. And what else do we do now?" Lorre reached down to help hold the baby and Jean began drying her as best as possible.

"We've got to get her warm, that's for sure. No telling how long we'll be here." She laid the t-shirt aside. "Hold the baby up." Her voice took on the same authority it had maintained during the delivery, and once again Lorre moved to comply with her command. He pulled the baby up very carefully and Jean unbuttoned her flannel shirt.

"Okay, now lay the baby down here on my stomach!"

Lorre placed the baby on her stomach and Jean buttoned the shirt around her, then pulled the coat up loosely over that. The baby moved her mouth toward Jean's breast and she quickly pulled her bra loose, allowing the baby to nurse. The baby stopped crying as she sucked, wheezing a little. She was already turning a ruddy color, losing her bluish-purple cast. Jean eyed the little girl, grinning, then suddenly she shuddered.

"What is it?" Lorre was alert to her movement.

"It's the afterbirth."

"Oh," he answered, as if not sure what she meant.

Jean needed to push and did so. The placenta came out quickly, with little effort compared to the baby. She looked back to Lorre, but he did not speak. "I'll have to get warm myself if I'm going to keep the baby warm."

She pushed herself forward holding an arm on the baby to stabilize her. Then working rapidly, she wrapped loose hay around the placenta and laid it to one side. The cord started to tangle again, and unflinching, Lorre helped her.

"I'd-I'd better get my pants back on," she said. Lorre nodded, picked them up and helped her slip them on. Her legs were cold. Lorre looked to Jean's face, but she was unconcerned. She smiled at the tiny head above the shirt.

"We'll have to do something about the cord," Jean said as Lorre started to relax. "It'll have to be tied."

"Uh, you mean that cord?" Lorre said, pointing to the one leading from the placenta.

Jean nodded. "Give me one of your shoestrings!"

He looked down at his shoes, then quickly undid one.

"Good," she responded. "Now, just wrap it around the middle there," she directed his movements with her eyes, watching carefully as he tied it. "Pull it tight. As tight as you can." He did. "Okay, now we'll leave it like that for the doctor to handle later."

"What does that do?" Lorre asked, looking down at his handiwork.

"It keeps any of the baby's blood from seeping back to the placenta. If the blood would seep out for some reason, the baby could bleed to death."

Lorre nodded.

Jean laughed then. "You know, you're going to be a medical expert before you're through with me."

Lorre laughed, too, and shook his head self-consciously, then slowly got to his feet. "My legs are getting cramped. Cold, too," he said. "You know, I really feel tired." He looked at his watch. "It's already after three."

"Did you sleep last night?" Jean asked.

"No. Been awake now for more than a day." He stretched and looked around. The light in the old barn was dimming. The storm was bringing on darkness faster than normal.

Lorre walked to the door, grabbed a handful of snow and gulped it. He ran a hand over the beard stubble on his face as he stood looking out. "The weather's still pretty bad." He turned and looked back at her as he spoke. "Wonder if the lights for this place are still hooked up?"

He walked slowly around, then located a switch. He flipped it on but there was no response. "Aw, hell," he growled, "why would a farmer leave the electricity on in a deserted farm?"

Jean smiled in response and followed his movements back to her side. She shivered and he did, too, rubbing again at his wounded arm. "Arm's getting little numb," he said. "In fact, all of me is getting a little numb. I'm cold."

He stirred at a small pile of hay with his foot and the sweet, yet musty smell penetrated Jean's nostrils. Lorre plopped down on a bale at her side and exhaled wearily.

"How cold do you think it is in here?" Jean was trying to wrap her arms more around the baby's body as she asked the question. The baby was quieting, already starting to sleep. Jean smiled as she settled near her breasts—a tiny face, wrinkled and red. Jean raised herself gently, pulled the coat from under her and placed it completely over her stomach to cover the infant.

"I dunno, maybe 30, maybe even colder," Lorre said, responding to her question. "The hay helps keep it warmer, sort of like insulation, I guess. It's got to be below zero out there, though." He jerked a thumb at the door.

"Maybe I better open some of these hay bales and get the hay around you," he said as Jean shivered again. "That'll help keep you warm, I think, unless you think it'd hurt the baby."

"No, no, fine," Jean nodded. "I don't think it would hurt at all."

Lorre began snapping strings off several of the bales and fluffing the hay over Jean's legs and around her body. He moved carefully, keeping a close watch on the tiny body on her stomach. Finished, he sat down heavily, several feet away, and leaned back against some bales.

"Do you think the baby's warm enough?"

Jean's eyes sparkled as she looked down at her daughter, who was now making a squeaking sound. "Yes, I think she'll be okay. I know she still feels warm to me. Let's hope some help comes soon, though. Rollie—my husband—should be on his way home by now."

She glanced at the door and Lorre sat up sharply. His relaxed expression of a few seconds earlier was replaced by a wary one.

"Do you think he might be delayed because of the storm?" Jean spoke quickly, trying to relax him again.

"Yeah, he might," Lorre replied nervously.

Jean stirred uneasily. She wanted Lorre to relax, but she wanted Rollie to come, too.

"Look, I'm sure he'll get through," Lorre said as she moved. "Those police cars are well-equipped for all kinds of weather. He'll just have to be driving slower, that's all."

Jean smiled. "Yes, I never even thought of that. How long do you think he'll be held up?"

"What time does he usually get home?"

"Oh, about two-thirty or three. Depends on how many reports he has to fill out first."

"Well, then I'd guess he'll get home somewhere between four-thirty and six," Lorre said. "Then he'll probably start looking for you."

"Do you think he'll know where to look?"

"Probably not right away, but how many choices has he got?" Lorre replied. "He'll probably check a couple of spots where you might be and then get some help out to look for you. Shouldn't be too hard. After all, there aren't that many roads around here. Besides, Jack's still there and he heard the name of the town where you said you wanted to go."

"But he'll probably be gone by now."

"No, I don't think so," Lorre answered. "I bumped him some with the truck and it looked like he was hurtin'. I figure he's still there, just trying to keep outa the cold."

Lorre shifted his position, then spoke softly. "Your husband'll be looking, all right, and he'll be finding us, too."

Jean eyed him questioningly, then leaned back and held the baby tighter. She knew Rollie would

144

first go on the hardtop road. It might be hours, maybe all night before he could get around to looking over this way and then finding them. She had to stay warm and keep the baby warm, too. She looked back at Lorre. He was watching for her reaction.

"Okay," she smiled gamely. "Guess we'll just hang in here then till he arrives. Right?"

"Right." He said it lightly, then leaned back again. "I guess I'll just plan on leaving you then," he glanced at his watch, "at, say, about five-thirty or six. That'll give me time to get away before your husband finds you. You'll be okay on your own here till then, won't you?"

"Leave?" Jean asked anxiously. "Why do you have to leave? I mean, you don't have to worry. I won't turn you in, and once my husband is here and takes care of me, you can leave then! Please . . . please Lorre." She paused, a look of panic on her face now. "Stay. At least till we see him come."

"No, I can't. He's got to know who I am especially after he finds Jack and talks to him. I can't afford to take the chance."

"Okay, I can understand how you feel," Jean interjected, "but what if he can't get through tonight? What if Rollie doesn't come? It's already getting dark, and I'm—I'm afraid to stay here by myself. Lorre, I need you, and so does my baby!"

Lorre looked to the baby and Jean tugged the shirt back. The little girl's head was turned toward him, eyes tightly closed. He sighed, then nodded. "Okay, I'll stay, but only on one condition. When your husband comes, I hide in the back part of the barn, and you tell him I left right after the baby came. I'll move on later. You've got to promise me that, or I'll have to go sooner." He stared at her.

"Yes!" Jean shook her head in vigorous agreement.

Lorre sighed again and Jean echoed it with one of her own and settled back.

The quiet of the barn absorbed them both. They lay there, covered by the hay, and listened to the wind as the light grew dimmer. Each was caught up in private thoughts. Finally, Lorre broke the silence. "You hungry?"

Jean looked toward him, startled. "No, not really," she answered.

"I am. I'm hungry and I'm tired. I guess losing all this blood is making me even more tired." He sighed for a third time and looked at the baby, then down to his hands. It was amazing, he thought, as he stared at his thick fingers. These hands helped bring that baby into the world. He looked back at her. Watch yourself, kid, it's a pretty rotten world. He coughed once. Funny, he felt dizzy. He shook his head to clear it, then looked at Jean. She was watching him.

"Hey," he said hoarsely, "you should try and get some rest, ya know. You'll need your strength for the kid."

"Yes, I know, but I've been sitting here trying to think of the right thing to say to you for helping me. I don't think I could have made it alone, and I'm grateful."

"Aw, don't worry, it's okay," Lorre answered self-

146

consciously. "I still can't figure how I even managed to help. I guess I've sorta always thought I was too clumsy and stupid to ever do anything that good. Now I've got this feeling . . . " he paused, "well, it's really unbelievable the feeling you get when you help do something like that, you know?"

Jean smiled gently. "I know." She looked down again at her baby, then back to Lorre, concern on her face. "What are you going to do about your shoulder? Is it still bleeding?"

He eyed it ruefully. "Yeah, a little. Hurts more than anything. I'm kinda glad it's cold. Helps ease the pain some." He looked around the barn. It was quiet inside. The howling wind reminded him of past storms, when his family was warm and safe inside, secure against their stove fire and later snuggled into their down beds. He chuckled and Jean looked questioningly.

"Just thinking about me'n a friend back home. We used to play in an old barn like this. Sort of a 'king of the mountain' thing with the hay and all. Sure was fun." He sighed. "Sometimes I wish we had never grown up. At the time I couldn't wait. Now I could wait forever."

"Yes, I know that feeling," Jean responded. "But there's a lot of important things for adults, too. Like having this baby, for example."

"Oh, I'm not sayin' that, but life was so much better for me then. The playing with my friends, the hunting and fishing with my father. You know, this may sound funny, but I once went hunting with my dad this time of year and it was a damn warm day.

It's funny the way each year changes. It's really funny. Hell, that one year, there were a million birds flying. Now, a day like this, they're probably all down somewhere freezing or struggling to keep alive.

"You should've seen where me'n Dad hunted once," he smiled. "It was a sight. There were all these birds headin' south and makin' a hell of a racket. And the geese. You should've seen those big Canadians, just winging across the sky in their big wide vees, calling to one another—free. God, they were so free.

"You know, when I saw those big, beautiful birds, I thought: Wouldn't it be something—to fly so high and so free? To look down and see the houses and fields and be above everybody and everything and know you could just fly on and on?" He stopped and looked at Jean. "Sorry. I didn't mean to go on like that."

"It's okay," she said it quietly and a small tear trickled down her cheek unattended.

"You know, it's really not so bad with this hay around you." His voice carried a lighter tone, trying to steer away from his past reflections. "If we think about it hard enough, we'll be so warm, we'll forget about all this winter and think it's a day of spring."

"Sure," Jean laughed. "Just forget about all that winter out there."

They sat quietly for the next few moments. Lorre contemplated the blizzard and what had just happened to him. Finally, Jean broke the silence. "You should give yourself up, you know. They'll be able to fix your shoulder and once I tell them how you helped me, I'm sure they'll take that into consideration, too. After all, if you hadn't been here, I probably wouldn't be alive."

Lorre was barely listening. He felt relaxed, drowsy. He had closed his eyes and now partially reopened them. The stacked hay was spinning around him. He shook his head, trying to clear his mind and respond. "No. I mean, going back now—well, it would be too hard. I've got to have some freedom now. It's what I've wanted. What I've been dreaming about for so long. All year—no, hell, all my life. It's like your new baby there. Would you want her to be tossed into a cage and grow like a trapped bird? I don't think so. And I don't want that either. I'm not saying I shouldn't be punished for a wrong, but for God's sake, give me a fair punishment. Don't let me rot in some damn prison!"

Jean looked steadily at his anguished face as if searching for her answer. "You said you loved life," she finally said. "Then how can you risk the chance of bleeding to death? You've got to try to help yourself."

"Why? Why should I? So I can go back to that cage? No! I love life, but without any freedom, then I guess it's over." The emotion was draining him further. He had to stop to catch his breath.

"Yeah, it's going to be over then," he said it softly, more to himself than Jean. "I'll have to find some peace somehow. Someone up there will understand what I'm doing."

"Then you'll let yourself die before you'll turn

yourself in, or surrender?"

"I guess so. But I think things'll be okay, don't you? I don't know why, but I've got this feeling. I think I'll be staying free."

Jean stared, silent, then shifted under the hay.

"Lorre."

He looked toward her.

"I hope so."

He smiled—a tired smile. "Me, too."

Jean smiled back, then snuggled back into the hay and closed her eyes. Lorre stared, glassy-eyed, at her for a while, transfixed by her look of peace and calm. Then he looked at his shoulder. The bleeding had stopped. He was tired. Very tired. Now was when he had to get some sleep if he was to continue his journey. He looked at his watch. Nearly four-thirty. A nap for now would have to do. The shoulder was throbbing, but the pain seemed farther away. He settled deeper into the loose hay and closed his eyes.

CHAPTER ELEVEN

It was six-thirty when the big plow burrowed its way into Rollie's driveway and cut a swathe toward the house. Even with the snow blowing as hard as it was, Rollie could see something was wrong. As they approached the house, he confirmed it—the door was wide open, sending a shaft of light onto the snow-covered porch. He slapped the driver on the leg. "Kill it and get down. If anything goes wrong, get the hell out of here!"

The driver slipped the machine out of gear and slid down onto the floor where he could still see the yard and house below. Rollie unsnapped his holster and stepped out quickly, clinking the door shut behind him. Mike materialized at his side, eyeing the open door. The police car lights blinked behind him. "What do you think?" He was unsheathing his revolver as he spoke.

"Don't know. But if they can see, they know we're here. We better stick together." Rollie pulled his gun free. "Come on, let's go!"

"Wait!" Mike reached out and grabbed his arm. "Don't you think we better call in—in case."

Rollie looked back, wild-eyed, then calmed himself and motioned toward the car. Mike hurried back to the cruiser. In seconds, he was back.

Not speaking, they crouched and advanced toward the door. The snow slowed them, but also provided cover. They worked their way to the porch, then pulled themselves up from opposite sides of the door. Sidling to the window, Rollie glanced inside. The room was a mess, but empty. He ducked below the sill and duckwalked to the door, then stood, back to the wall. Mike aped his position on the other side.

"Okay?" Rollie looked to his partner and sucked in his breath. Mike nodded. Together, they crashed into the room, quickly deploying inside on either side of the door, guns ready. They were greeted by silence and signs of a fight. There was blood on the floor near the largest of the room's three chairs.

Rollie looked worriedly at his partner. Mike motioned him on and positioned himself at the corner of the couch.

Crouching lower, Rollie moved to the kitchen door and looked in. It, too, was empty. He shook his head at Mike then edged on to the bedroom. Cautiously turning the handle, he pushed, then dived inside. Nothing. He slowly stood. "Okay, let's check upstairs."

Mike waggled his gun and Rollie opened the

152

stairway door while standing aside. It was black. He paused for a split second, flipped the light switch, and took the stairs two at a time. Like the rest of the house, it was deserted.

He rushed back down the stairs and checked the back door. The snow indicated no one had come through recently. He walked back inside, confused, then spotted the severed telephone cord. He held it up in disgust, then looked worriedly toward Mike.

"Look, you sit down a sec, okay? I'll get on the horn about this." Mike put an arm out and guided Rollie to the couch, pushing him firmly down. Stepping outside, he signaled all clear to the plow driver, then started for the car.

Rollie sat for a few seconds, then leaped to his feet. "The shed!" He jumped to the door and flicked on the yard light. The force of the storm could be clearly seen against the lone bulb's glare.

"Mike!" he shouted through cupped hands and saw his partner stop just short of the car. Rollie waved him back and Mike came on the run.

"What—what is it?" He puffed from his sprint.

"The shed. They could be there!"

Rollie pointed to the outline of the building, barely visible in the darkness.

"Okay, let's check it," Mike said.

They trudged toward it, guns still drawn. The plow driver, seeing their movement, ducked down again as he watched them advance. Their breathing came in gasps, iced over by the sub-zero air.

"Damn!" Rollie stopped the advance with his curse. "The door's open. They must've taken the truck!" They moved on toward the gaping black hole on the shed's side. Near the wall Rollie could see the faint impressions the tires had made, although they were nearly filled with drifted snow. They stopped short of the old building, then gingerly dodged inside. Kneeling along the inside wall, Rollie found the light switch. The sudden illumination revealed nothing. Only the old feed bunks cast shadows back at him. He stood and breathed a long, slow sigh.

Mike stood, too, still puffing. They looked at the tracks together, silent. Mike stepped out and kicked at the snow. "Must've pulled out several hours ago, way it looks. They couldn't have come our way though, or we'd have seen them. Besides, the snow was packed in so bad they'd have been hung up somewhere. You think they took the road to Marion or headed north?"

"I don't know. Christ! Mike, they've got Jean." Rollie looked at his partner with horror-filled eyes. "They wouldn't hurt her! You don't think they'd hurt her? Not in her condition. Good God, don't let them hurt her!"

"Hey! Take it easy, man. It'll be okay. They probably just have her as a hostage. They're just scared. Quit panicking, man, you're going to have to help. We can't afford to have you going off the deep end. Now, come on, let's get this called in and get some help out here. Give me a description of your truck." He slapped Rollie on the shoulder. "Pull yourself together, man, and let's go."

"Yeah, okay," Rollie felt numb. He leaned back against the wall and quickly recited the truck's description. His stomach was churning. He started to sit down, but Mike was already on the way out, so he turned and stumbled behind, dumbly ignoring the stinging snow.

A sudden blast from the snow plow's horn brought him back and he looked toward Mike. Another blast. Both men broke into a run, nearly falling in the deep drifts. Rollie could sense the driver's urgency as the horn sounded a third time. Rollie reached the plow first and the driver dropped down beside them. Mike stopped short, bathed in the arc of the plow's headlights.

"What . . . what is it?" Rollie, gasped, trying to catch his breath. His lungs hurt from the short run.

"Well, I ain't real sure," the driver replied. "I just got down and stepped off to the side there . . . I really had to go, you know, I got pretty weak kidneys. . . ."

"Okay, okay," Rollie cut him off impatiently. "What were you on the horn for?"

"Well, I don't know for sure, but I think I saw a body back there." He pointed toward the far corner of the house.

Rollie's heart jumped and Mike held up a cautioning hand, signaling Rollie to keep cool. They moved forward cautiously, past the plow's lights, then past the car. They were out of most of the lights' range when they saw the dark form nearly covered with snow. Mike moved forward first, pushing Rollie back. "It's a man," he shouted. "He's frozen stiff. Must've been here a while."

Rollie breathed a sigh of relief, then moved

forward to where Mike was kneeling. "Think it's one of them?" He put a hand out and touched the corpse.

"I don't know. Let's get him up to the porch and see." Mike started to pull the frozen body upward, Both men saw the gun then, locked in his death grip. Mike let the body fall back, then pried the weapon free. "It's a police revolver." He handed the gun to Rollie who shoved it in his pocket. "Come on, let's move him."

They lifted the body and carried it to the porch, into the light. Rollie brushed snow and frost from the man's face. It was a bluish-white color, the mouth twisted, a grimace of pain showing at the edges. The corner of his frozen mustache was matted with dried blood. Mike pulled the coat open and began checking the man's lockets. Rollie stared at the clothes. They were his.

Mike was working down the man's legs, then he stopped, pushing at the right foot. He wiggled the loose shoe, then pulled it off. "Thought it looked swollen," he muttered as he eyed the bandaged foot. "This is probably where that blood in the house came from. Looks like he was shot. Don't see any other bullet wounds, though. The left side of the body looks like it was caved in. Remind you of anything?"

Rollie looked, felt the left side, then pushed the man over on his stomach. "Yeah, just like that hit-and-run job we took on 90 last summer. Think he was run down?"

"Well, he was smashed hard by something. Something big. Could be that's what killed him.

Hey, look here!" He pulled the waistband of the man's underwear. "Prison issue." He shivered as the snow swirled over them.

"Yeah, he's got to be one of our boys, all right. And the other one's got Jean and the truck. God. . . ." Rollie stared at his friend's face, then away into the night.

"Look, you just wait here while I get a call in. Okay?"

Rollie nodded.

Mike hustled back through the snow to the car, and Rollie stood and surveyed the house, then glanced back to the dead man and finally to the dark, snowswept sky. He walked to the door and carefully pulled it shut, making sure he heard the latch click before starting back toward the plow.

The driver was still standing alongside, stamping his feet to keep warm. Mike joined them there. "Well, where shall we try first?" he shouted, pounding his hands together.

"They must've took off for Marion on 21! We'll head that way! The only other through road is that gravel about three or four miles north of here!"

"Maybe I'd better get a unit on that one, too!" Mike yelled.

"Well, maybe," Rollie hesitated, "but I doubt they'd head off there. Jean wouldn't steer him toward that road. Not in this. You can call it in if you want, but I'd bet they're either on the way or already at Marion. Maybe even past there. I'll stay with the plow and you follow!" Rollie was already climbing up on the passenger side. "Come on! Come on! Let's not waste any more time! That guy's got my wife!"

"Okay, but I'm going to get a car on that gravel, anyway!" Mike shouted up. "Rollie, take it easy. We'll find them!"

Rollie sat tensely in the cab, gripping, then regripping the revolver, which he had still not returned to his holster. He sat silently, not answering the plow driver's questions or initiating conversation on his side. He nearly went into a trance watching the swirling snow as it rolled wavelike from the plow's curved blade into the blackness. Rows of blinking red and amber lights suddenly loomed out of the darkness. He stirred, the trance broken, and looked over to the plow driver.

"That was quick. You made good time."

The driver looked back. "Yeah, half hour or so. Guess it was pretty good."

"Half. . . ." Rollie shook his head in disbelief, then checked his watch. Seven-forty-five. Jesus! He'd lost an hour. He looked forward again as the driver slowed the plow. The lights now firmed up as three police cars, straddling the road. Rollie pulled open his door and climbed out.

"You see anything?" A man in police garb advanced toward him, shouting the question.

"No."

"We're wasting our time out here then. Let's get on into town and out of this wind." He turned to walk back to the cars.

"Wait!" Rollie hurried to his side. "Is this all that's being done? I mean, isn't some sort of search going on in town?"

"How the hell should I know?" The man looked tired as he turned back. "I'm not directing the operation, just following orders. I thought it was a waste of time setting up this block in the first place. Hell, they're probably frozen solid somewhere by now."

"No they're not! We need to get this search going!" Rollie shouted excitedly, grabbing the patrolman by the arm. "What kind of a damn setup is this, anyhow? I want to talk to whoever's giving your orders!" He was screaming hysterically, waving his gun in one hand while grasping the man's arm even tighter.

The policeman stepped back, eyeing him warily. Two others started toward them, noticing Rollie's actions. One unsnapped his holster as he walked.

"Rollie!" Mike reached out and took him by the shoulders, spinning him around. "What the hell's wrong with you? Get your senses together, man!" He waved off the tired officers and pulled Rollie toward the plow. Rollie looked back over his shoulder, but relaxed slightly. Mike placed a hand on the gun and pushed Rollie's hand down.

"Put that gun down and get back here! Man, you're going to get yourself put away with any more of that." He pushed Rollie ahead of him, past the plow and onto the passenger side of the car, motioning for him to get in. Rollie slid the gun back into his holster and got inside. "Stay there!" Mike commanded, walking quickly back to the plow.

He climbed up the passenger side, shouted

something to the driver, then jumped back down and ran back to the car. Ahead, the three patrol cars were already swinging into line for the trip to Marion.

"Now, listen," he said, getting in on the driver's side. "I want to find Jean and that goon as bad as you do. But you know as well that those guys don't know any more about the search plans than we do. You've gotta stay rational, man, or you'll eat away your mind worrying."

"Yeah, yeah, all right," Rollie answered, staring down at the floor. "It's just that I, well, I *am* worried—about Jean. You know. Jesus, Mike, what if-if she's dead?"

"I don't know. But I'll tell you this, you're not going to help her or the search by tearing into every guy who says he isn't sure what's going on. Now either settle down and work at this logically or, by God, I'll have you locked up myself until you get your senses together! Where the hell's all that calm and cool I've been watching these past few months? We're all beat, man. It's been a long, hard day. Believe me, those guys are working their butts off to find some answers for you. Don't screw it up." He pursed his lips determinedly, then shifted the car into gear and moved forward to catch up to the plow already trailing into Marion behind the trio of patrol cars.

Rollie looked straight ahead, silent, then turned toward his partner. "Okay," he said hoarsely. "I'm sorry. I'll try to make it easier. It's just that I'm," he paused, "I'm afraid. Mike, I'm afraid." Tears welled up in his eyes as he continued staring across the seat at his friend. "I'm afraid for Jean, and I'm afraid for me. God!" He shuddered. "What'll I do if she's dead?"

Mike glanced across at him, then answered with reassurance. "Look. I understand. I really do. But don't think the worst. As far as we know, they're safe somewhere—maybe even here in Marion or up the road at another town. Keep the faith, man. Things'll work out."

Rollie swiped a gloved hand across his face, then snuffed loudly. The street lights of the city were around them now, and he tried to compose himself as they approached the downtown section. The police cars and plow had pulled up in front of a large brick building and Mike guided his car into line behind them. He stopped, shut off the engine, then looked back at Rollie. "You okay?"

"Yeah. Let's get inside." They stepped out into the snow and trudged toward the building marked City Hall.

"I think the wind's dying some," Mike said, looking up at the street light above them. "Snow seems to be slacking off, too." He shivered. "Cold isn't gone, though. Must be 20 below."

They stamped up half a dozen steps and into the building. The three officers and the plow driver were standing together with two other members of the Marion Police Department and a gray-haired man sitting behind a desk. They looked up collectively as Rollie and Mike entered, paying particular attention to Rollie. He walked forward to the man with whom he had argued. "Look, I'm sorry. For out there. I, uh, wasn't thinking right. Day's getting to me, I guess."

The policeman eyed him for a few seconds, then smiled faintly and held out his hand. "Yeah, well, that's okay. Guess we all get a bad day."

Rollie shook the hand, then sank down into a chair. It became apparent that the gray-haired man was running the show. Rollie sat back, barely hearing the conversation even though he looked up attentively from time to time finally listening as Mike said, "Okay, so you want us to head out north, right? As long as we can keep that plow, we'll be fine. Yeah, yeah, I got it."

Rollie stood, looking to Mike for direction. "Come on, we better get on the road." Mike jerked his head in signal and Rollie fell in behind him, heading for the door.

"Oh, and Chief," Mike turned back and Rollie nearly ran into him head on. Mike looked at him impatiently, waiting for him to step aside, and Rollie obliged. "Chief," Mike repeated, getting a clear view of the gray-haired man again. "You'll keep us posted?"

"Don't worry. You'll know when I know," the chief answered, waving them on as he picked up the phone.

Mike tugged at Rollie's coat to urge him along. They walked back outside. The wind and snow had dropped appreciably. It was bitter cold, but the feeling of a total blizzard was dissipating.

"Good," Mike said. "At least we ought to be able to

see better and keep the roads clear once they're opened."

Rollie looked around. "Yeah. Should help all right. Uh, where we headed?"

"North, on old 37, just like the man said," Mike answered. "Rollie, you sure you're gonna be okay? I can take this alone and you can hang in here with the chief. I'm sure they'll get you right in on anything that comes down."

"No, no, I'm fine. I'd rather be with you—in case. Don't worry, I'm ready anytime you are."

"Good. Then let's hit it." Mike yanked open the driver-side door and signaled to the plow driver to pull out. The driver waved and climbed back into the plow cab. Within moments they were traveling rapidly through the deserted streets, heading north, once again toward open country.

"You think they might have gone this way?" Rollie loosened his coat, leaning back as he talked.

"I don't know, but it's as good a chance as any," Mike replied, glancing down at the speedometer, then readjusting the heater controls. "The only thing that's sure is that your truck hasn't been spotted anywhere here or in Hollysberg. The others will look west, so we'll take this road."

"What about 37 south?" Rollie asked quickly.

"Good God, man, weren't you listening back there? The chief said south 37's been shut down all day. They've had a repair crew on that street, rerouting traffic on west around town. He figures if they did come through and try south, they'd just continue west once routed that way. It's a big hassle getting back to the south access."

"Oh," Rollie answered, peering back out front. Now they could see nearly as far as the lights' arc. The snow was definitely stopping.

"Zebra Nine, this is Marion."

Rollie grabbed for the mike with both hands, nearly breaking the holder as he jerked it free. "Zebra Nine." He croaked out the words, his hands trembling as he held the mike between them.

"Yes, Zebra Nine, we have a sighting on the Patterson truck. . . ." Mike flicked on the spotlight and began signaling the plow driver. " . . . One of your units from Hollysberg reports spotting the truck on County Road 129, approximately twenty-nine miles northwest of Hollysberg. Are you aware of that location?"

"Ten-four," Rollie whispered. "Mike, it's the gravel road north of our place. Goddamnit, why didn't I think they'd go that way—all this time!" They pulled to a stop behind the plow as Rollie dropped his hands and the mike to his lap. The he jerked them back up, depressing the talk button.

"What about the occupants? Any report on the occupants?"

"Negative, Zebra Nine." A wave of static cut in over his voice and Rollie fumbled for the squelch button to cut it back.

"Could you repeat that, please, you were cutting out."

"Yes. There's no report on the occupants. The Hollysberg unit says the vehicle has been abandoned."

CHAPTER TWELVE

Jean woke with a start, looking wildly around and almost sitting up. The movement and whimpering from her stomach stopped her motion and she glanced quickly down, then remembered. She sighed, then settled back, hugging her baby in the process. It was very dark now in the old barn, and she had trouble focusing, making out the baby's face only after staring intently for several seconds.

"There, there, everything's going to be okay," she cooed as the baby started to cry and move her head. Jean pulled the baby's body toward her chin and the tiny mouth came to rest on her breast, then began sucking. "Yes, my little darling, yes, everything will be fine."

She held the baby closer. An intense feeling seemed to bond her tightly to her new daughter. It was a closeness she'd felt with no one before, not even Rollie. She lay quietly, barely breathing as she watched. "Yes . . . everything will be okay. . . ."

She looked up toward the barn door, trembling and wondering again if indeed everything *would* be okay. The wind's howling was the only sound, and even that seemed quieter than before. She was surprised at how warm she was. Piling the hay around her had been a good idea.

She glanced over at Lorre, now easier to see as her eyes became more accustomed to the dark. He was covered with loose hay and lying still. She couldn't make out his face, but decided not to call to him, in case he was not awake. She felt very sorry for him. If only I could do more to help him, she thought. Maybe another talk after he woke would convince him to turn himself in for medical help. She'd just have to try.

She adjusted her hips and winced. She was stiff and sore. She wondered what time it was, then moved again. She wanted to get up and find a place to go to the bathroom, but she also wanted to remain where she was, not disturbing her warmth or the baby. She opted for the latter. I can wait yet, she thought, looking again at the tiny head nursing at her breast. It would be a difficult maneuver when she did have to move and she wanted to put it off as long as possible.

The baby squirmed on her stomach and she laughed. It tickled. She watched intently at the baby's sucking. She wished there was something she could eat. She thought about it more, and the more she thought, the hungrier she got. Wonder what time it is? Lorre had a watch. She thought again about calling to him. No. She would wait and watch. When he moved, she'd ask.

She stared toward him, trying to think him awake. Nothing. Then, almost as suddenly as she'd found it, her newfound energy and hunger waned. She lowered her head again, feeling drowsy. She yawned and looked at the baby, then pulled her coat up tighter around her.

The baby's eyes were closed and she'd quit sucking. Jean pushed her carefully away from her breast and pulled the shirt back over both the baby and herself. She began moving rhythmically back and forth with her upper body, humming softly. Now how does that song go? She wrinkled her forehead. "'Bye baby bunting, daddy's gone a'hunting." Rollie would already be hunting. He'd find them before the night was through. She was sure.

It took the plow only half an hour to reach the spot where the Patterson truck sat partially buried. A darkened patrol car was already on the spot and a flash from its spotlight was the only indication it was occupied. The plowman cut his lights in response and Mike followed suit. Rollie was out and running almost before Mike had pulled the car to a halt.

Although the wind was still kicking up in gusts, it had died to the extent where the snow was settling. What snow was in the air was only there from the wind action.

One of the patrolmen advanced to greet Rollie as

167

the latter hurried to the side of the truck. Rollie grunted in response and edged carefully forward to the driver-side door.

"It's empty. We already checked it before we called."

Rollie waved him back, running a hand over the cracked door window where the bullet had connected. Yanking open the door, he stood back, surveying the windshield's damage. He pulled his flashlight free from his belt and flicked it on. Aside from the bullet holes, the interior looked normal. He played the light across the seat, then onto the door. It was stained. He leaned forward, peering at it intently. "There's blood all over this door," he said, stepping back. "Did you see the blood on the door?"

The officer shook his head, then stepped forward to look, taking Rollie's light. "Yeah, it's blood all right. Driver must've been hurt."

"Ummm," Rollie responded, looking up toward the buildings at the far end of the drive. Mike and the other patrolman had joined them now and they followed Rollie's gaze.

"We've been holdin' off checking that till you could get here. Didn't know if we'd need a backup or not—and besides, uh, we figured, since it was your wife, you'd want to, well, uh. . . ." The patrolman looked to Mike for help.

"Yeah, glad you did," Mike answered quickly. "Okay, let's check it out. And Rollie," he stepped in front of his partner, "we'll take things slow and easy. Got that?"

168

Rollie looked angrily at his partner, then stared back toward the barn, which blocked out most of the other buildings with its size. "You think there might be a house back there?"

"Might. It's hard to tell what's back there with that damn big barn in the way."

"Yeah," Rollie answered, trudging forward, loosening his gun as he moved. Mike hurried ahead, watching Rollie out of the corner of his eye and staying beside him.

"Rollie, slow down. Use some sense or you'll get us all killed!"

Rollie stopped and turned toward Mike. "What the hell do you want me to do?"

"First, let's check out the barn. And move up slow. If they're in there, we're setting ourselves up, and Jean could get hurt. If that guy's wounded, he may shoot first and not give us a chance to talk him out. If we just go marching up there, we'll sure as hell get our heads blown off!"

Rollie held his position, lips pursed in anger, then sighed, his shoulders sagging in the process. "Yeah, okay." He nodded, looking again toward the barn, still a good fifty yards away. "You got a plan?"

"No. No plan. Just some common sense. There's four of us. If we split up here, we can take the barn from two sides and get a look at the rest of the place at the same time. If there's a house, we'll take the buildings first, one at a time. We can start with the barn."

"But we can't just go busting in there," Rollie interrupted. "I'd rather let the guy get away from there if it means not taking chances with Jean." The other patrolmen joined them, shivering and rocking back and forth on their feet to keep warm. "Look, once we're up there, let me try calling Jean's name. If she's there and okay, she'll answer, or at least that con will. Then we'll know where we stand, right?" He looked at his partners for affirmation.

"Yeah, and maybe neither one will answer and we'll have to hit it anyway," Jim, the driver of the other car said. "But I figure by now he knows we're here, so what the hell." He shrugged.

"All right," Mike answered. "Jim, you guys take the rear and give us the high sign when you're in position. And don't do any shooting unless the guy comes out alone. Make sure your shots are on if you take any. We don't want any stray bullets hitting Rollie's wife."

Jim nodded and they moved away to the left, plowing into the deep snow toward a small grove of bare trees. The sky was almost clear now, but its blue-black color made it hard for Rollie and Mike to follow the other pair's movements. Finally the men reached the trees, then crouched, leapfrogging forward toward the barn's rear. They stopped short of the building and signaled.

"All right. Easy." Mike stepped off, then down into the small ditch on the left side of the driveway. Rollie stayed along the right side, not walking in the ditch but crouching as he went. Mike struggled through thigh-deep drifts, then climbed back up along the driveway's edge and followed Rollie's lead.

There were no signs of footprints along the drive, but an occasional hard gust from the wind provided the reason why. They reached the long side of the barn and Rollie edged out, taking the farmstead. Two other buildings, no house. He scrambled back to Mike's side. "No house. There's two other smaller buildings. The door for this one's about halfway along that west side. There's some sort of entrance on the far corner, too."

"Okay, let's move on up. I'll stay back by the corner to cover and you try calling Jean. But watch out for anything and move if he shows. I'll be marking on your back. Remember, these guys already killed back at the prison, and this might be the one who pulled the trigger!"

Both men were gasping as they spoke. The air was bitter cold, and the ache had returned to Rollie's lungs. He nodded and walked back toward the corner of the barn, while Mike turned and signaled their intent to the others. He hurried to the corner to join Rollie.

Aside from their labored breathing, the men made no sound. The snow, still powdery, muffled their movements. Mike dropped to one knee at the corner and braced his left arm along the barn's wall, gripping his gun in both hands and training it on the center of Rollie's back.

Jean snapped her head up and looked around. Something had awakened her, but she wasn't sure what. She looked at Lorre. He was still lying peacefully in the same position she had last observed

171

him. Then she heard Rollie's voice.

"Rollie! Rollie, is that you? I'm inside. . . ." She stopped as Lorre moved, staggering to his feet. He was having trouble maintaining his balance. She could see the fear on his face. "Rollie, wait! Don't come in. Wait!" She looked up at Lorre. "He's here! You've got to get back in the barn now!"

Lorre lurched, zombie-like, toward the barn's rear, reeled several steps forward and fell. Jean screamed as the barn door flew open and a shadowy figure dived inside. She looked again toward Lorre. He was crawling forward, breathing heavily.

"Rollie?" Her voice was almost a whisper as she looked to where the shadowy figure had entered.

"Jean! Where are you?" The words were terse, quick.

She could see him now, crouched behind several bales, gun pointed over the top in her direction. "Over here. I'm over here. To your left."

Rollie turned toward her voice and edged forward. He stopped as Mike jumped in through the still-open door and dived into a pile of loose hay. Rollie continued creeping forward. Lorre got to his knees and moved behind several bales. Jean jerked up, clinging tightly to her baby as she saw Rollie tense and aim his gun up at the movement.

"Rollie, don't. He's one of the convicts, but he's been shot. He's in real bad shape." Lorre was gasping, fighting to get his body turned toward them. She watched him out of the corner of her eye as she reasoned with her husband.

"Rollie, he can't fight you. He can barely move.

172

You've got to help him. He helped us. He helped deliver our baby!"

"What?" Rollie stared at Jean, startled. She pushed back the coat top and leaned forward, displaying the baby's head.

Mike advanced to several feet behind Rollie. "Jean . . . are you okay?" It was Mike asking the question. Rollie remained transfixed.

"Yes, yes, I'm fine. We're both fine, but we wouldn't have made it without Lorre—the convict." She looked back at him. He was half-draped over the bales, still breathing hard and keeping his gun aimed in front of him. His gunhand was trembling. "He's been shot and has lost a lot of blood," Jean continued. "The other convict shot him while he was trying to help get me to the doctor."

Rollie took a deep breath, then stood. "You ready to give yourself up?" He shouted toward Lorre's position.

"No," Lorre replied hoarsely. "I'm not going back."

"Rollie, don't listen to him. He's delirious," Jean cried.

Lorre groaned and pushed himself up on the bale, finally standing, his legs wobbly. Rollie dropped to one knee at the move, training his gun on Lorre.

"Lorre!" Jean screamed. "You've got to go back! You've got to get your shoulder fixed!"

"I. . . ." He wavered a little, but kept his gun up.

"All right!" It was Rollie again. "Drop that gun and come forward slowly or we'll shoot." He clicked the hammer back on his gun as he spoke.

"Rollie, no!" Jean looked at him, horror-stricken.

Mike, too, stood up at Rollie's threat and asked, "Are you crazy?"

"I know how to handle an arrest," Rollie spat back at him. "This man's a dangerous killer."

"He saved me, and the baby," Jean sobbed, not believing it was her husband speaking this way. "Lorre," she pleaded, struggling to her feet, guarding the baby, "please. Come with me."

"No, it's too late." He started to step forward and Rollie pulled up to shoot. Jean screamed as Mike dived and hit Rollie in the back. The gun exploded; the bullet went harmlessly into the ground.

Lorre looked at Jean, tears in his eyes, then crumpled to the ground. She screamed again and dropped to her knees at his side. His eyes were closed. Mike left Rollie and ran ahead, quickly rolling Lorre onto his back and putting his head on Lorre's chest.

"Jean, he's dead." Mike looked up, then reached out and put a hand on her shoulder as Rollie stepped up beside them.

"Would he . . . have had to go back . . . to prison . . . even though he helped me?" she stammered sadly.

Mike nodded.

She sighed. "He told me that more than anything, he wanted to stay free, no matter what it took to get it. Maybe. . . ." She let the sentence trail off and looked at Lorre's face. It was calm.

"Come on," Rollie urged. "We better get you to the doctor. God, giving birth in a barn!"

There was a noise at the door, and the other patrolmen rushed in. A gust of wind followed them, carrying snow in over the people inside. Several flakes fell onto Lorre's hair and face and Jean reached out and gently brushed them away. She held her hand to his face for a second more, then pulled it back.

"Yes," she whispered to the baby. "We'd better get you to safety. It's time for us to go."

Rollie helped her to her feet, but she pulled away and moved ahead of him into the clearing, cold night. She stopped, breathed deeply, clutched her baby tighter against her breast, then started toward the patrol car. The tears were already freezing to her face as she walked.

THE END